The Rancher's Unexpected Bride

A CHRISTIAN MAIL-ORDER BRIDE ROMANCE

MALORY FORD

Contents

Chapter One

September 1885

Paige Brown stepped off the train in Mud Lake, Colorado, with a pep in her step and hope in her heart. Finally, she'd managed to get out of New Orleans, and the memories it held. The relief she'd felt at Mara's innocence being declared felt like bricks lifted from her shoulders. She'd had the chance to help right a wrong and help the sister who had sacrificed so much for her, but the anticipation of what came next had the butterflies in her stomach turning to seagulls.

Riding with Liam and Mara had kept her from letting her mind run away with the "what-ifs," but they joined the excitement now. Being a mail-order bride was never something she expected she'd do, and now she wondered if she'd made the right choice.

What if Riley found her lacking?

What if they couldn't stand one another?

What if he wasn't as good a man as everyone thought?

Shaking her head to dispel the thoughts, Paige refused to think of worst case scenarios. Both Kate and Mara were in Mud Lake, and they'd built lives for themselves that felt so different from how they'd all grown up - orphans abandoned and abused until Hope House scooped them up. Both of them became mail-order brides as the fastest way to escape New Orleans safely, but they'd fallen in love in the process. She could do the same.

The mountains which provided the backdrop to the dusty road and town center had her jaw dropping, as did the lack of oppressive heat she'd left behind in New Orleans. It was only the first of September, but already she could sense a fall which wouldn't be knocking on Louisiana's door for months yet.

An elbow poked her side, and Paige turned to her big sister, Mara. "It's like this place is from a storybook."

"It is," Mara replied with a smirk. "But I want to make sure you're certain about this. Riley's a good man but-"

"But nothing. You've spent your entire life sacrificing for me, and it's time I forge my own path." Unfortunately, life in the West meant she'd come to Colorado as a mail-order bride, but so had Mara and Kate. They'd married the Pratt brothers and promptly fallen in love with them. If the two of them could, why not her? Softening her tone, Paige did her best to show compassion for her sister's protectiveness. "You've gotten me this far. Let me do the rest."

Mara's husband, Liam, who was Mud Lake's sheriff, grinned. "Welcome home, ladies."

"It's beautiful."

"Wait until you see the actual lake," Mara replied. "The folks who settled this place were mighty sneaky to keep it from becoming overpopulated."

"I can see why." Paige glanced around, shielding her eyes with her hand. "Any idea where I might find my groom?" Riley Hart, a hardworking and God-fearing man according to Liam, was the foreman at the Pratt ranch. Neither had known he'd sent off for a mail order bride, but it had all happened rather fast according to Mrs. Miller. Glancing at the satchel in her brother-in-law's hand, a rush of nerves ran up Paige's spine as she thought of the creamy lace concoction Mrs. Miller had sent with her to wear when she married. It was real, and she was less than a day from meeting her groom.

"His sister and brother-in-law run the mercantile, so let's stop there first. If he's not there, he's out at the ranch, and I'll be happy to take you out there. The mail here sometimes gets delayed, so don't let his absence make you nervous." Liam's words calmed Paige a little, but nervous energy had already begun to build.

"That's all right. I know things happen. I'm just happy to not be all alone up here." Turning to Mara, Paige clasped her hand. "I know you're on edge with me marrying, but thank you for respecting my choices."

"Like you said, you're a grown woman." Mara glanced up at Liam, and he chuckled. Paige had no idea what he'd done, but Paige knew she had Liam's reassurance to thank for Mara's lack of argument. "As for your health, if you have any episodes, please let me know. We have a good doctor here, and I plan to inform him of your condition."

Paige bit back the urge to snap at her sister, but then Mara had been managing Paige's lung condition from the time they were on the cusp of adolescence. It wasn't consumption, more like something the doctor had called asthma, but he'd been unwilling to prescribe such a young girl the experimental treatments they had. As such, she'd had attacks every few weeks since childhood, but it was never anything she couldn't handle. "I'll handle it. Now, we've got more exciting things to do."

The mercantile was just as charming as Paige might've imagined, and she could see her sister's touches of organization in the place despite her only having worked there a short while. Mara had always been the more organized of the two, and she was one of those odd ducks who enjoyed spending hours upon hours cleaning and finding places to put things.

Before she could give voice to her thoughts, a squeal sounded just as Kate Donovan Pratt ran from the back room of the building. "Your train was early!" She barrelled into Mara as another woman with a long blonde braid followed her. "When Liam wired you'd been cleared, I think I spent a solid three hours thanking the Lord. And Paige, I can't believe you're finally here." Kate's eyes glistened, but the clear joy on her face was contagious. Mud Lake clearly agreed with her friend, and Paige could only hope it would agree with her as well.

The blonde woman behind Kate stepped forward and hugged Mara. "It's so nice to meet you, Paige. I've heard such good things about you from Kate and your sister. I'm Lizzie Gaines. I run the mercantile with my husband, Paul."

"Well," Liam snorted. "Apparently you'll be getting to know her well."

The bell above the door jingled to punctuate Lizzie's curious expression, and three tall, broad men stepped through. All three wore Stetsons, and the man in the front grinned wide as he approached. "You're back. Kate had me bring her in first thing this morning, and we just made a day of it with a supply run."

"Paige," Kate said with a huge grin as she settled into the cowboy's side. "This is my husband, Samuel, our foreman Riley, and our wrangler, Joshua. I can't wait to have you out to the ranch. Oh, do you know where you'll be staying? The Olsens are here for a few more weeks, but-"

"I guess that's more of a question for Riley," Liam interrupted. He grinned at the slightly taller and thinner cowboy behind Samuel. The man's hair matched his sister's, but his brows furrowed in confusion at Liam's words. "Why didn't you tell us you sent off for a bride?"

Had a pin dropped, they'd have heard it as everyone's mouths dropped open in shock. Paige felt her cheeks pink as the heat rose up in them, but she pasted a smile on her face. Stepping forward to the handsome blonde cowboy with wide amber eyes, she extended her hand. "Pleased to meet you, Riley. I'm Paige Brown, your mail-order bride."

Riley Hart was more than handsome if she was being honest. His blonde hair was cropped closer than Liam's. He didn't have the beard Samuel had, but she could see small wisps of hair sticking out from the bottom of his Stetson. He was at least four inches taller than her five foot seven inches, but maybe more like five or six. A little thinner than the Pratt brothers, his shoulders were still broad with strength she imagined came with the manual labor he did everyday.

"I...I..uhh..." Riley's words came out on a stutter. "You're my...what?"

For the first time, embarrassment and true worry flipped her belly. Had he not gotten Mrs. Miller's letter that he'd been matched? Did he find her so repulsive he couldn't imagine marrying her? Before she could speak again, Liam broke the silence. "Riley, you did send off for a bride, didn't you?"

Feeling a brick of dread settle in her stomach. Paige was certain she knew the answer before Riley even spoke. "No," he said with a pained expression. "I didn't. But-"

As though they had a mind of their own, words fumbled from Paige's mouth. "All right then." Could they hear how close she was to tears? "Mara, you told me there was a cafe in town that might be hiring. Could someone direct me there? Is there a boarding house in town?" She turned to Liam, too afraid to look at the sure pity in her would-be intended's eyes.

Blessedly, Liam didn't push. Paige wasn't sure she could handle much longer in Riley's presence without bursting into tears. "We sure will. And there's no boarding house, but there are a few widows who might rent out extra rooms."

Of course, her sister had no such confidence. "No, she can-"

"Darlin'," Liam replied in a tone Paige knew would diffuse her sister. "She can do this."

"Wait," Riley spoke up finally. "How did this happen? And I may not have sent for a bride, but that doesn't mean I won't take care of her. She shouldn't be alone out here." He shoved his hands in his pockets, and the beads of sweat on his forehead almost made Paige feel bad for him. "I mean...I'd be willing to..."

"No," she said with every bit of conviction she had. If Riley hadn't sent for a bride, she'd not be turning his world on its head through no fault of his own. She'd not accept a dime from the man if she could help it, and for once, she truly would make her own way in the world. "You don't need to do anything. I'm not alone here, and I don't intend to trap any man into marrying me." Remembering the letter, an inexplicable need to nail the coffin shut on the idea of her marrying him rose. She pulled it from her pocket and handed it to him. "So this isn't your handwriting?"

What was her intent there? She honestly didn't know, unless there was some irrational hope he'd suddenly remember writing the thing. It was a shame. He did seem like a good man, and he'd been willing to take care of a woman he didn't send for. That had to count for something in his favor, right? Still, she'd been honest when she said she'd not trap him. She could do this - she'd have to.

His amber eyes pained, Riley shook his head. "It's not. You can ask my sister." His gaze met hers, and she held it. His clear apology and regret over the situation diffused the rest of her ire. Riley handed the letter to Lizzie, and she looked equally chagrined. "It's not. I'm so sorry. But Liam's right. There are definitely folks in town with extra rooms. We can help ask around to see if any would be willing to rent them out."

At a poke in his ribs from Kate, Samuel spoke up then. "If it doesn't work out with Stew at the cafe, you're welcome to stay at the ranch. It would be a bit of a trek to come into town everyday to work, but we've got room." Despite having had to be jarred from his surprise by his wife, his offer did seem genuine. Still, being at the ranch everyday would undoubtedly mean seeing Riley often. She wasn't angry at him, but she didn't know she could deal with the humiliation.

She nodded, plastering another smile where the other had slipped. Mara took her hand, and she gave it a squeeze. "Thank you. I appreciate all the help."

"Come on," Mara said. "Let's go see a man about a job."

Riley had never felt more like dirt on the bottom of someone's shoe in his life. Well, he had, but that had also come with a heavy dose of fear and need to get out of Boston. This time, as he watched Paige's figure retreat down the street, the guilt was punctuated with anger. "Who could've sent that letter?" His words came out on a growl, and his teeth threatened to crack as he ground them together.

"We don't know," Samuel said calmly. "But you've got to keep your head to figure this out. She's all right, and Liam will make sure she stays safe here."

Kate snorted, the first bit of levity in a sea of tension. "If he gets there before Mara. She shot a man once to protect Paige in New Orleans, and I doubt she feels a lick of guilt about it."

What in the world? He'd known Liam's wife was feisty, so it really shouldn't be a surprise. Still, why had she needed to shoot a man for Paige? What had Paige been through in her life that he'd just added to through no fault of his own. "I don't know what to do, but I have to help her. She came here to marry me. She's my responsibility."

"Riley," his sister's gentle voice said. "She doesn't seem to want your help, and it appears she's confident in that decision." She studied him, sisterly understanding in her eyes. "I know you worry about folks you care about, but she has others who care about her and can help. Besides, the way to a woman's heart is never by viewing her as a responsibility."

Her heart? Lizzie had jumped about ten spaces, but she didn't understand. None of them did. They couldn't. One woman's death was already on his hands, and he'd not be the cause of another to come to even a lick of harm. Paige was beautiful, with her dark blonde hair and strikingly attractive features, but none of that could be his focus at the moment.

For the first time since they'd entered the mercantile, Joshua spoke up in his southern drawl honed in Tennessee. "I wonder if she'd marry me if I asked. You didn't send off for her, but I'd been thinking about it when I saw what good matches Samuel and Liam got. I could take care of her, and it ain't like she came here intending to marry someone she knew." He shrugged, oblivious to Riley's clenched fist. "A wrangler don't make quite as much as a foreman, but I've got plenty to build a cabin."

It made no sense at all, but the idea of Joshua moving in on Paige in her vulnerability grated him to his core. "Stay away from her," he said in as even a tone as he could manage. Joshua was a good man, but the last thing Paige needed was one more vulture swooping in as soon as they heard she was single.

Brows raised, a smirk rose on the wrangler's face. "Message received, brother, but you know I'm not going to be the only one with the thought - especially when they see her."

"Gentlemen," Kate cut in from her place at Samuel's side. "Allow me to make a suggestion. Paige seems intent on making her own way, but she can use all the friends she can get in town." Her scrutiny settled on Riley. "Befriend her, and see where things go. Don't go treating her like a china doll on a shelf or something to be claimed. She won't take kindly to it."

She was right, and he knew it. "I'll go try and talk to her." Maybe, just maybe, he could use friendship to convince her to accept some help. The idea of Paige meeting a similar end as Alice turned his stomach, but there was no way he could explain it. Rather than try, he pushed out the mercantile door and jogged down the street towards the restaurant. No, he'd help Paige get to a safe place, and he'd lay out any man who thought to swoop in and take advantage.

Chapter Two

"Thanks, Stew," Paige said as she shook her new employer's hand. "I won't let you down."

The red faced man with a round belly and sweat dotting his forehead studied her. "No, I don't reckon you will. Pay comes every Friday, and you'll work the breakfast and lunch shifts. Your sister says you can cook, so I'll put your skills to the test this week. I'd prefer you stay in the back so I don't have a riot on my hands of fellas coming in to flirt with the pretty new waitress."

He spoke so matter-of-factly Paige wasn't the least bit nervous, but the idea of causing a stir in town brought heat to her cheeks. "I'm sure they'll get used to the new girl in town soon." She couldn't afford to lose this job due to trouble.

Stew shrugged, removing a rag from the pocket on his apron and wiping his forehead. "We'll see, but if any of 'em give you trouble, come talk to me. I don't brook any nonsense, especially towards my staff."

Finally able to take a deep breath, Paige took in the dimly lit restaurant around her. The large windows in front let in a good bit of light, and both the tables and tall counter and stools were empty for the moment. It was mid-afternoon, so she imagined it would fill up soon. "I'm sure it'll all be grand, and I don't mind working the dinner shift as well." Goodness knew she could use all the money she could get.

"Nope," Stew said quickly. "Pretty soon, it'll get dark right around closing, and I'd rather you not be walking home after sunset by yourself. Speaking of which, where are you staying?"

That was a good question, as Paige hadn't gotten that far yet. "Your guess is as good as mine for the moment, but I'm hoping the pastor and his wife will have a spare room I can use for a few weeks while I find more permanent accommodations." They'd offered to house her when Mara first arrived, but since then Pastor Harold had decided to retire. The new pastor, whoever he was, would need the parsonage.

Just then, the faint smell of bread moving from perfect to overbaked reached her nose. "I think your bread needs to come out," she said without thinking. "I'm sorry, I'm sure you've got it handled." Had she just offended her new boss before she even started? Biting her lip, Paige prayed he was as easy going as Liam seemed to think.

Stew's eyes widened, and he rushed towards the kitchen. "That's quite the sniffer you've got on ya, girl. A few more minutes, and my dinner customers would've been eating dry sandwiches." Tossing the loaf pans on the counter, he shoved the towel back in his apron. "Go on out, and find a place to stay tonight. I'll see you at half past six tomorrow."

Grin wide on her face, Paige bid him goodbye and made her way back outside. Liam and Mara stood in a sweet embrace, and her brother-in-law kissed Mara's forehead just as she realized Paige had emerged. "Well?"

"I'm hired! I start tomorrow morning for the breakfast and lunch shifts." Clapping her hands together, she took a deep breath. "The Lord's taking care of me." Breathing a prayer of thanks, she didn't miss the knowing glance Liam sent her sister's way.

Her mood didn't last long, however, as Riley jogging down the street had her knitting her brows together in confusion. "What else could he have left to say?"

Liam shrugged, wrapping an arm around Mara as he did so. "Not sure, but we'll give you two some space to figure it out." Mara opened her mouth to argue, but a quick wink from Liam had it snapping shut again. "Have him walk you over to the parsonage when you're done. We'll introduce you to Pastor Olsen and his wife, but I'll let you ask about accommodations." He smirked, and Paige couldn't believe how lucky she'd gotten in a brother-in-law.

"I will." Just as Liam led Mara away, Riley reached her but didn't speak for a moment. He appeared to be looking for the words. That was fine, as it gave her a chance to study his features a little more. His jaw was strong, and she had the sense that when he smiled it would light up his whole face. Those eyes, the color of a wheat field just before harvest, swam with unspoken thoughts.

"Paige," he started as he shoved his hands into his pockets. "I'm sorry for how this has played out, but I want you to know I'll take care of you. Even if I didn't send a letter off to Mrs. Miller, you're my responsibility." He paused, eyes clenching shut. "I mean-"

Holding up a hand, Paige shook her head. She'd been a burden to others since she was a child, and there was no world in which she'd simply transfer the burden from Mara to the man before her. A wanted mail-order bride was one thing, but an unwanted one? No, that wasn't a role she was willing to fill. "Riley, I'm not your responsibility." Could there possibly be a less romantic statement?

"It's not your fault I'm here, and I've already gotten a job with Stew in the restaurant."

His shoulders tensed, and his gaze shot to the small building where she'd be spending most of her time. "You're waitressing? I don't know if that's a good idea. Some of the miners can be a little rough around here."

Forcing herself not to snap at his assumption he had a say in what job she did, Paige clasped her hands in front of her. In the calmest tone she could muster, she chose her words carefully, though her ire was clear in her tone to anyone who listened. "It's clear you're a man who takes his responsibilities seriously, but I'm not one of them. I've accepted a job as a cook, and I'll thank you to keep your opinions to yourself in the future. Now, if you'd be so kind as to direct me to the parsonage, I'm meeting my sister and Liam there."

***

With a sheepish wave at Paige as she stepped through the cheery front door of the parsonage, Riley tilted his head back with a heavy sigh. Could he possibly have handled that any worse? But why was she so unwilling to accept help from him? She'd stay with the Olsen's, but she'd not allow him to lift a finger?

The creak of the front door alerted him to its opening a second time. Stepping out onto the porch, Liam had a knowing smirk which Riley briefly wished he could wipe off the man's face. "So, that clearly went well."

"What tipped you off? Was it the way she barely said a word to me as I dropped her off, or the way she didn't even look back to wave goodbye?" He removed his Stetson and ran a hand through his short blonde hair. Still trying to calm himself from the last hour, he took another long breath. "How did this happen? What kind of person would send off for a bride for someone else, knowing good and well they had nowhere to house her and no idea she was coming?"

The smirk fell from Liam's face, and he shook his head. "I don't know, but I'm hoping I can find out. Paige was lucky she had family here, but it could've gone much worse if she'd truly been alone. I don't know if it's some hateful lover of chaos or a well meaning matchmaker, but I'm planning to write to Mrs. Miller to see if she'll send me any information she had from who she thought was you." He shoved his hands in his pockets, studying Riley intently. "How are you doing with all this?"

How did he even begin to answer that question? "Honestly, I feel like I just got thrown off a horse in the middle of a stampede. I know I didn't react as well as I could've at first..."

Liam shook his head. "I think, under the circumstances, you reacted as well as any man could've. Though I wasn't present for your conversation outside the restaurant, so the jury's out on that exchange." His lip twitched again as he raised a brow expectantly.

The sun had already begun to fall behind the mountains, and crickets started to sing their nightly song. Sounds traveled down the street from the livery as folks began to return rigs and horses they'd rented, and Lizzie stepped out onto the mercantile porch to sweep up from the day. It all felt so normal, as though his whole world hadn't just been upended.

"I basically tried to strong arm her into letting me help her."

With a snort of laughter, Liam nodded knowingly. "And how'd that turn out for you?"

"About as well as you'd imagine. I feel responsible, Liam. I can't help it. Once I got over the initial shock, it was like something in me needs to make sure she's taken care of."

Liam closed the distance between them and placed a hand on Riley's shoulder. "That's because you're a good man, and the more Paige gets to know you, the more she'll see it. But these women from New Orleans won't be controlled. Paige's stubbornness might be wrapped up in a more cheerful package than her sister's, but they've been through more than you can imagine. Plus, Paige saw Colorado as her shot at making her own way in the world the best she thought she could. She's been taken care of by Mara since their parents died, and she's intent to solve her own problems."

"How am I supposed to just walk away when all anyone ever says is how a woman ought not be alone this far west? You know what nearly happened to Kate when Samuel was just across the street." His gut flipped at the thought of Paige getting cornered by miners so starved for a woman's attention they'd take it by force if they had to. "I won't let that happen to her."

Expression serious once more, Liam stepped back and studied the street as well. Most of the miners who milled about were good men, but the ones who weren't would drool at the sight of her gentle southern beauty. Goodness, even Riley had been struck dumb by it initially, and he had only respectful intentions.

"She'll be fine," Liam said. "I'm in town, and so is Paul. We'll look out for her, and you know Mara's going to fight tooth and nail to have an armed escort with her wherever she goes." He winked, but the truth of his words remained. "I'm going to talk to Stew as well, and Mr. Olsen knows his way around a pistol if need be. I understand the feeling of wanting to keep your woman safe, but if there's one thing I've learned about these ladies, it's they're not helpless."

His words made sense, but one phrase didn't settle well. "She's not my woman."

"No, she's not," Liam said with a chuckle. "Just like Mara's not really mine and Kate isn't really Samuel's. They all belong to the Almighty, and He's a whole lot better at working out sticky situations than we could ever be. I saw her strength in New Orleans, her determination to clear her sister's name. The Lord gave her that, and He'll help her here too." He paused before continuing. "But don't think for a minute I didn't see the way you looked at her in the mercantile. You may not have sent off for her as a bride, but there's a part of you that wishes you had."

Before Riley had a chance to respond, Liam tipped his hat and turned on a booted heel to head inside the parsonage. What could he have said, anyway? As much as Riley would prefer not to admit it, Liam was right. Still, he had no choice but to take his advice and trust the Lord with her safety.

As Riley made his way back to the mercantile where he'd tied his horse that morning, the sight of Donnie Gray's strut had him stifling a groan. He didn't need a run in with the guy, not when he was already a breath from planting his fist into something as it was. Coming closer, Donnie adjusted his Stetson which was far too clean for anyone who'd done any actual work.

"Evening, Hart." Donnie's drawl told of his parents' southern roots, though he'd lived in Colorado most of his life. Liam and Samuel had dealt with his nonsense from the time they were children, but Riley had mostly been able to steer clear of the too-big-for-his britches dandy who wanted everyone to believe he was a cowboy. "Who was that pretty little thing with Pratt and his wife?"

"None of your concern."

Something flashed in Donnie's eyes, and Riley feared he'd just ignited the beast of competition in him. From what the Pratt brothers had told him, Donnie had always thrived on competition, the thrill of the win far more important to him than the prize. With the Gray family money they'd brought with them from Tennessee, he'd often won.

Riley would never forget watching the defeat on Rupert Gunderson's face when Donnie had outbid him for a prime spot of land to build a family ranch simply because the man had initially worked at the Grays' ranch. He'd left because the apple didn't fall far from the tree when it came to Donnie's father, but mostly because it was time he struck out on his own. Thankfully, Samuel had helped him procure a spot of land a little east of Mud Lake, and the family seemed to be doing well.

Still, Donnie's thirst for competition couldn't be sated. "She looks a little like Pratt's wife, but her hair's darker. Reckon she's got the same fire?" Were they walking over to the Olsen's?"

The tension in his jaw almost painful, Riley narrowed his eyes. Donnie didn't even attempt to mask the predatory glint in his eyes, and his hands remained relaxed in his pockets. "Don't go near her. She's not interested, Gray."

"We'll see."

Refusing to dignify Donnie with a response, Riley shook his head and pushed past him to the mercantile. Lizzie's husband, Paul, stood on the front porch, hands crossed over his broad chest as his light red hair looked a little more auburn in the sunset's light. With brotherly compassion clear on his face, he studied Riley as he approached. "You all right? You took off mighty quick earlier."

The crickets had kicked up, and more than a few folks finished closing up their business. "I'm fine, but I don't really know where to go from here." At least that much was true, though "fine" was probably an overstatement - especially after his run in with Donnie.

Paul nodded, not pressing the matter any further. "We're always here, brother. Let us know if there's any way we can help."

A little more of his ire faded at that, though the simmering fear he'd be responsible for the pain of another woman continued. "I appreciate that. Let Lizzie know I'll be by later this week to take the munchkins off your hands for a few hours." One thing about having to leave Boston Riley would forever be grateful for was the relationship he'd been able to have with Lizzie's kids. His niece and nephew somehow set the world to rights no matter how upside down it seemed.

"Will do."

Chapter Three

P aige grinned at the kind older miner who'd just wiped his plate clean with a fervor which could only be described as desperate. "I'm so glad you enjoyed it." It was her third day at Stew's restaurant, and so far she'd been going back and forth between cooking and waitressing. The constant change of pace was nice, and it suited her well. "That gravy recipe has been passed down for at least three generations." She winked, but the familiar pang which always followed when she thought of her early childhood in the kitchen with Mama threatened.

"That right there is gold on a plate," the man said with a voice which sounded a little like a wagon rolling along a gravel road. "Stew," he called a little louder to the back where her boss clanged around with pots and pans. "I think this little gal is gonna put you out of a job. Not only can she cook, but she's a country mile better to look at."

Paige laughed, not the least bit offended as the man didn't say it with even a lick of disrespect. "Maybe, but Stew runs the show here, so I think I'll just learn from the master."

Wiping his hands on his apron, the man in question approached from the back. "Rhett, if you're just going to come in here and cause trouble, I'll be sure to add a little extra cayenne next time you stop by." His eyes twinkled, and he approached the table as well. "In fact, I might just do it anyway to be ornery." He playfully elbowed Paige in the side. "It pays to be the only restaurant in town."

Just then, Stew's smile fell into something between a scowl and suspicion as a young cowboy walked through the door. Paige hadn't seen him that she knew of, but his clothes were decidedly cleaner than all the other cowboys in town. His gaze found her instantly, and a sneer disguised as a grin split his face. "So you're Stew's new girl," he said with a low drawl. Boots clapping on the floor planks, he stopped about six inches too close for polite greeting and extended his hand. "Donnie Gray, ma'am." He removed his hat, something most of the men in town didn't appear to bother with.

"Paige Brown," she replied coolly. It was important to be polite to the customers, but the man before her sent an altogether unpleasant sensation up her spine. Even Riley's scowls and growls were preferable to the way Donnie appraised her now. In fact, she couldn't help but wish Riley was here at the moment. He might've made her madder than a cat on washing day, but she felt safe with him. Extending her own hand to clasp his, the lack of calluses there told her just how much work he did. In fact, hers were probably rougher than his.

Stew crossed his arms over his chest as Paige tried to release her hand from Donnie's. His grip firmed just enough for her to be unsuccessful, and her eyes narrowed. Before she could speak, her short, round boss did so on her behalf. "Come on, Gray. I'll get you seated. Paige was just about to head back to the kitchen."

Annoyance flickered over the cowboy's features, compounded when Paige jerked her hand back with more force than necessary. "I think I'd prefer Miss Brown to serve me."

If it hadn't been before, his intentions and character came into clear focus in that moment. Paige might not have had as much fire as her sister, but she'd grown up on the same streets. "Too bad, it's my turn in the kitchen. I can assure you, you'd rather me be cooking than serving." It was true, as Paige was still getting the hang of keeping all the tables straight when it got crowded. Cooking, on the other hand, was something she could do blindfolded.

As though she'd not even spoken, Donnie shifted to stand beside her and placed his arm on the small of her back. "Come on, Paige. I can be a generous tipper."

Bile rose up in her throat at his insinuation, and she stepped away from his touch. Just as Rhett and another miner who'd come in for lunch stood from their seats, Paige spun to face Donnie. "Are you hard of hearing, Mr. Gray? Or do you simply suffer from a short memory? Either way, you should probably get that checked out with the doc. As it stands, I'll be heading back to the kitchen, and Stew is more than capable of getting you settled."

She moved to step around him and walk toward the kitchen, but he shifted his feet and she was met with the wall of his body. "Excuse me?" Pointing to Paige, Donnie turned his attention to Stew. "Are you going to let your girl talk to me that way?" His attention back on her, Paige swallowed down the urge to step back at the fire in his eyes. "I'm not a man you want to cross, Paige."

The last of her control snapped, and every bit of the street kid she'd been rose up in Paige and tumbled out of her mouth. "First, Mr. Gray, I'm a grown woman. I can speak for myself, and I haven't been a 'girl' in years. Second, it's Miss Brown to you." Summoning every bit of courage she possessed, she stepped just far enough around Donnie to hit him with her shoulder on the way by and made her way to the kitchen. She'd gambled Stew wouldn't fire her over the offense, but his expression had been murderous from shortly after Donnie came in.

A small shuffle sounded in the dining room, followed by Stew's voice. "Don't even think about it, Gray. You're no longer allowed in my establishment, and if I see you again, I'll send for the sheriff. I know he'd relish the opportunity to lock you up for the night."

With a glance over her shoulder, Paige spotted both Rhett and the other miner who'd stood to his feet guiding Donnie towards the door as Stew shook his head. As her boss turned to face her, a little fear she'd just gotten herself fired for being rude to a customer surfaced, but she couldn't regret her actions. "Stew, I-"

"Don't you dare apologize," he growled. His face had grown red as a tomato, and she worried for a moment he might crack his teeth clenching his jaw so hard. "In my establishment, you'll be respected. Anyone who pushes that even a little will be thrown out on their behind, and if you need to smack somebody with a skillet, by all means."

Rhett pushed back through the door and approached as Stew spoke. "That go for me too? I got a couple men I'd like to take a skillet to." He shrugged, but his humor did seem to calm her boss a little.

Another minute of good natured ribbing between the two appeared to do the trick, and Paige spent the rest of the lunch rush in the kitchen letting out all her frustration over the encounter with Donnie the only way she knew how. For as long as she could remember, the marriage of structure and creativity in the kitchen had calmed her like nothing else. Sometimes, she prayed. Other times, she sang softly to herself. Quiet was always welcome as well. It didn't matter, as long as she could work with the raw ingredients in front of her.

Any lingering nerves from her encounter with Donnie melted away as she seared chicken, worked bread dough, and got creative with sauces and sides. The smells lifted her spirits as they wafted to the ceiling, and she was so distracted she didn't even hear her sister shove through the front door and hightail it back to the kitchen until the woman was within swinging distance.

"Paige," Mara said breathlessly as she came to a stop next to the stove. "There's been a fire at the Pratt ranch."

Head whipping around to her sister as she instinctively took the skillet off the hottest part of the stove, Paige's heart dropped into her stomach. All the peace she'd felt moments before came to a screeching halt as she thought about what that could mean for Samuel, Kate, Riley, and everyone else who lived on the land she'd not even seen yet. "Is anyone hurt?"

"I don't know. Liam just tore out of here a few minutes ago to go help, and Paul's rounding up as many able bodied men as he can to go help. I was expressly instructed to stay here but..." Mara trailed off, and Paige knew exactly where this conversation would end up.

"Come on," she said as she wiped her hands on the towel she'd used to touch the pan. "Let me tell Stew what's happened, and we'll go see how we can help."

"No need," Stew shouted from the front of the restaurant. "I'm closing up early to go out and help too. The Pratt's have been mighty good to me over the years, and I won't let that spot of paradise they've got go down without a fight."

The reality of his words sunk in, and Paige's gut churned further. "Let's go." As they cleared out the restaurant and refunded anyone's meal who wasn't yet finished, an image of Riley heroically fighting the blaze popped into her mind. *Lord, I barely know this man, but I care about his well being. Not to mention, this is the Pratt's family land they've worked so hard for. Guide us, Lord, and help the fire not spread any further.*

Riley grabbed another bucket from Joshua and doused the west end of the ranch house as the rest of the hands worked to wet the ground all around the barn. The barn was a goner, but thankfully the blaze hadn't jumped towards the dry grasses of the pastures. Kate continued pulling the goats into the small pasture where Samson and Starlight generally stayed, as well as Rue, the milk cow. She looked exhausted, but Riley had to give his boss's wife credit. She never once complained as she'd taken on the task of getting every single one of the animals to safety.

Thankfully, the herds were a few hundred yards away, and the wind was so mild that day it barely even drove any smoke in their direction. As he handed the bucket back to Joshua, his hand smarted something fierce, and he let out a quick breath at the pain.

Samuel's head popped up from where he shooed the last of the goats after his wife. "You all right, Hart?"

Of course, he'd heard. His boss had the hearing of a bat. "I'm fine, boss. A spark just got me on the hand when

I was pulling Rue out of the barn." That wasn't exactly true, as the rope Clarence had used to bring her in for the afternoon was still attached and had begun to catch fire like a candle wick. Riley had torn it off before the fire could reach the cow, but he knew he'd have a nasty burn to show for it.

It was better than it could've been, and Riley thanked the Lord for that. The barn may need a complete rebuild, but he knew better than most how quickly a fire could take the souls of innocent people. The memory of the blaze aboard the *Sonia* would forever be burned in his mind, a far deeper wound than any he'd accrued trying to save as many as he could.

Still, part of the reason for that wound was the fact he'd forever blame himself for the deaths, and the "what ifs" regarding Randolph Shipping would always have him looking over his shoulder. At least this time, no one had been hurt.

The sound of horses and wagons drowned out any further thought, and he swallowed down the pain in his hand as he spotted at least ten men coming down the road from town. They moved with purpose, and his spirits lifted a little. Liam led the charge with Paul not far behind, and he realized the buckboards had folks crammed in the back. What he'd originally thought to be ten men was actually more like twenty, a testament to the Pratts' lives here and the town's desire to help.

"Here they come," Samuel shouted as he tossed another bucket of water around the perimeter of the quickly burning barn. Kate returned from getting the goats secured, and Riley could see the relief in her shoulders before she even spoke.

Clarence clapped his hands together and rubbed them, a grin on his face. "The cavalry's here, boss! Praise the Lord!"

Despite the circumstances, Riley found himself smiling as well, particularly since the fire was well on its way to burning itself out. The men jumped out of their wagons and grabbed buckets of water the hands had been bringing from the spring, and Riley finally had a moment to take a deep breath.

Unfortunately, the blood pumping through his veins slowing meant the burns on his hand could be fully felt. Shutting his eyes and steeling himself for the pain, he pulled his burned and tattered glove off, gritting his teeth to keep from shouting at the spots where the glove stuck to his hand.

The angry red on his palm had already begun to blister and bubble, some of the smaller ones pulled open as he'd removed his glove. Before he could study it further, a familiar voice cut through the fray. "Oh my goodness,

Riley," Paige said quickly. "Let me help you with that." She coughed a few times into her dress sleeve but seemed fine overall.

He wanted with everything in him to argue, but he couldn't bring himself to speak now the pain had fully set in. Glancing up, he realized Paige wasn't alone as Mara glanced at his hand as well. "Kate has some salve that'll keep it from getting infected," the elder sister said quickly. "I'll meet you both on the porch with everything we need. Paige, you probably need to move away from the smoke."

Surprising him, Paige took Riley by the arm and led him towards the porch. She coughed a few more times, but it dissipated quickly once they'd moved further from the barn. He'd ask about it later, but for now there wasn't much he could do.

The pain in his hand had grown more and more pronounced, so he didn't speak save a grunted, "Thank you," as she guided him to a rocking chair. His pride pricked as she did so, but at the moment he couldn't bring himself to care. Something about her being so close felt right, and the way she held his hand gently and studied the ugly red skin had the pain battling for top attention in his brain.

"This looks bad, Riley." She didn't sound disgusted or faint but actually leaned in closer as the front door opened and Mara stepped onto it with Kate trailing behind.

Mara took one look and went pale before placing the bowl of water, soap, towel, and salve on the ground. "Riley, I'd love to help you, but I've got a bit of a weak stomach for things like this." She turned around, and her tightened shoulders almost had Riley smiling. "I'll go get some more bandages while Paige gets you cleaned up."

Paige snickered and turned a grin on Riley which had him forgetting the pain entirely for a moment. Her big blue eyes contrasted with her hair which seemed to move between dark blonde and light brown depending on the light, the sun catching the tiniest bit of auburn as she caught its rays. "She's never been great with blood or other medical things, but she pushed through when she had to for me growing up. I'll never forget the time I cut my finger open gutting a fish down at the river. She convinced the tenement doc to stitch it up for me, but first she'd had to clean and wrap it up."

As she spoke, she'd set to work cleaning Riley's hand with gentle dabs and gently pulling dirt and rope fragments from the wound with tweezers he hadn't noticed Mara brought. It stung, but it wasn't nearly as bad as it could've been. "But she managed?" Hearing the fiery older Brown sister had a weakness brought a smirk despite the situation, and he did his best to focus on the story.

"She managed, though she was mighty green during the whole process. I was sure she'd swoon, and I'd have two medical emergencies on my hand." Paige pulled the last of the fragments from Riley's hand, dabbing it again with a soapy cloth. Tossing the first rag to the side, she took up another one and poured an amber liquid onto it. With a glance up at Kate, her brow rose. "How did y'all get hold of iodine out here?"

Apparently not as affected by the sight of Riley's hand as Mara, Samuel's wife knelt beside Paige. "I asked Doctor Collins for some a few months ago. There are too many small accidents on the ranch the hands refuse to go into town for. Basically, as long as the limb is still attached, they figure it'll heal on its own." She rolled her eyes. "Cowboys, you know. Anyway, Doc added a crate of it to his last supply run for us, and we pay him for it. It helps keep the wounds clean, if nothing else."

"Smart," Paige said as she dabbed the liquid onto his hand. "And what's in this salve Mara brought out?" She picked up the jar and sniffed it, the strong scent traveling to Riley already. "It smells amazing."

Kate smiled, clearly lost in a memory as she studied the jar of white cream. "Clarence makes it, and Samuel's mother taught him how. It's got a goat's cream base, and there's garlic, calendula, lavender, clove, and thyme.

I think he puts some willow bark in there for pain and swelling as well."

Paige sniffed it again before spooning it on to Riley's hand. With another breathtaking smile, she met his eyes again. "You'll smell better than any cologne for a few weeks until this heals." She winked, and Riley found himself going a little breathless at the sight. The thought he could be married to this woman if he'd just kept his big mouth shut that day at the mercantile crept in, but he shut it down. No, a lie was never a good foundation on which to build a relationship, and he wasn't sure he could bring himself to marry anyone anyway.

After what had happened aboard the *Sonia*, he'd put Samuel's overprotectiveness to shame. Paige deserved sunshine and wildflowers after the life she'd had growing up, and there was a darkness in Riley he didn't know if he'd ever be able to shake.

"Here it is," Mara said as she stepped back onto the porch with her eyes firmly fixed on the porch ceiling. Liam followed with a grin, his wife's discomfort clearly amusing. "I've got two rolls of bandages, but I'm realizing that's probably overkill."

Paige laughed and took the bandages from her sister's hand. "Probably, but we appreciate the thought." Over the next few minutes, Paige finished getting his wound wrapped, and he realized the rest of them had made themselves scarce. When had that happened?

"Where'd you learn wound care?"

She shrugged, tying off the last bit of bandage. "When you're on the streets, you've got to learn the basics. Then, at Hope House, the kids tended to come to the kitchen for help when they got hurt. It was probably because we always kept the cookie jar full, but I learned from one of the house mothers how to comfort the children as well as dress their cuts and scrapes."

An unbidden image popped into his mind of her holding a sniffling child in a small cabin with a view of the Pratt ranch out the window. The boy had her brown hair, but as he looked up at Riley, amber eyes took him in. Blinking his eyes to dispel the image that would help nothing, Riley took a deep breath and stood to his feet. He offered his good hand to help Paige to her feet, realizing just then how close they stood. "Thank you for everything."

She swallowed, her blue eyes unreadable. "You're welcome." She stepped back a half step, and he tried not to regret the extra space. "I'd...I'd better go see if Kate and Mara need any help with the animals." She paused, her voice coming out stronger this time. "Clean your hand with soap and water once a day, and some extra iodine won't hurt either. Use the salve, and make sure you put fresh bandages on every time. If it starts to get red or you start to feel feverish, get to town and go see the doctor immediately." With that, she turned on her heel and all but scurried inside the house.

Riley stared after her longer than he'd care to admit but was jarred from his thoughts by Clarence's gravelly chuckle from the ground beside the porch. "Looks like things may work out after all." With a little pep in the old man's step, he left before Riley could even respond to his musings.

Chapter Four

M rs. Olsen placed her fork on her cream colored
china plate that evening and wiped her mouth
with her napkin. "I'm so glad no one was hurt, but I hate
Samuel lost his barn." Paige agreed with her gratitude, but
also that of the fact her breathing episode hadn't been
worse than it had. She hadn't thought about it until they
reached the fire, but the smoky air was one of the things
which typically triggered her mostly mild asthma. As soon
as her throat started to itch and her chest started to feel
heavy, she'd moved into cleaner air. She wasn't the only
one struggling with the smoke, so no one had commented
about it.

The Olsens had been just as kind and generous as everyone said they'd be, happy to house her until the new pastor

moved in next month. It gave her a little time to find someone else to board with, and it allowed her to save a few paychecks since they'd insisted on taking no rent. She was fairly certain Liam had given them a little money for food, but no one had expressly mentioned it. "I know. It could've been much worse."

Pastor Olsen took a sip of his water. "Heard Riley got himself burned pretty good, though. Did he mention it to you?"

"Actually, I'm the one who helped clean and dress it." Pink rose to her cheeks as Mrs. Olsen's eyebrows rose. "The others were so busy, and Mara can't stand the sight of such things, so I jumped in to help." In reality, the moment she'd seen Riley's angry flesh, she'd not given it a moment's thought. She'd been honest when she told him about her experience with patching folks up, but none of the small cuts and scrapes the children got beckoned her with quite the fervor Riley's wound did. Perhaps, it was the severity of it, but she wondered if it had to do more with the man himself.

Pastor Olsen nodded approvingly. "Samuel said he got it when he ran into the barn to get the milk cow. He even went against a direct order from Samuel to do so, as he didn't want anyone but him running in. It's a good thing, because to hear Samuel tell it, by the time he'd gotten back from getting Starlight and Samson to safety, the barn was caving in."

The thought of Riley in the barn when the place crumbled down around him turned her stomach, but she did her best not to show it. "The Lord was with them all today."

"He sure was," Mrs. Olsen said. "That Riley Hart - he's a good man." Her eyes twinkled a little at her words, but she didn't say anything else.

"He's from Boston originally, right?" That was all she knew about him, as she'd not invited much discussion about him from Mara or Kate when she saw them.

Pushing his chair back, Pastor Olsen placed his hands on his thick belly. "He is, but no one really knows what brought him out here. He used to work for a shipyard according to Lizzie, but he more or less showed up on her doorstep a few years ago and hired on at the Pratt ranch that week." He shrugged. "I reckon a man is entitled to share whatever he wants about himself, but I'd be lying if I said I hadn't wondered a time or two."

Interesting. Did he have a criminal past no one knew about, or was it more like Mara and Kate's situations in which he'd been the victim of unfounded accusations? "I guess you're right, and I'm glad he seems happy here."

Mrs. Olsen scowled at her husband, though the love in her eyes was clear. "Honestly, Hal, you gossip worse than any biddie in this town."

"What?" The pastor's grin told Paige this wasn't the first time they'd had this conversation. "She's his mail-order bride, and I didn't share anything Mara and Liam wouldn't have said anyway."

Mrs. Olsen whipped him softly with her napkin and stood from the table. "She's not his mail-order bride anymore. She's making her way in this town how she sees fit, and she doesn't need you filling her head with idle gossip." Turning back to Paige, she shook her head. "Don't mind my husband."

Chuckling, Paige realized what a gift she'd been given staying with the Olsens' for these few weeks. The two of them bickered and groused, but they clearly had deep love for one another which came only with the passage of time. Even now, after he'd been thoroughly scolded, Pastor Olsen watched his wife leave the room with a smile on his face. He lowered his voice and whispered conspiratorially. "Sometimes, I say these things because she looks so pretty when she's riled."

Mrs. Olsen's voice carried from the kitchen. "I heard that, Hal."

"I meant for you to, dear." Then, he stood from his own seat and gathered the remaining dishes at the table before turning his attention back to Paige. "I'd better go offer to do the dishes before I end up on the couch for the evening."

As he followed his wife, shoulders bouncing with mirth, Paige watched the two of them sharing the load of cleaning up. That right there - the simple joy of coming home to someone who loved you and the happiness of playing together even after all those years - it was everything she wanted in a marriage.

Lord, she prayed silently as she took her own dishes into the kitchen. *I don't want to desire things that aren't in Your plan for me, and I trust Your plan is best. Still, I need You to help me remain content no matter what that plan may hold.* In a frustrating but not unexpected moment, her prayer ended with a thought of a certain ranch foreman's face. She couldn't help her thoughts, and it only served to send her back into prayer committing herself to the Lord's plan for her. Whatever that plan was, it was certainly better than any path she'd stumble into on her own.

Flexing his injured hand outside the church that Sunday, Riley thanked the Lord again his injury hadn't been worse. Overnight, the pain had begun in earnest, but the salve Clarence made worked wonders as long as he applied liberally.

Memories of Paige's sweet face as she applied it the first time assaulted him again, and he did his best to put it from his mind. He had no business thinking about any woman as much as he had Paige, particularly one he had no commitment to. It would probably be best to try and avoid her, as he couldn't seem to keep himself from letting her weave her way into his thoughts and dreams.

Just last night, he'd jolted awake from a dream in which Paige had been in the barn when it caught fire. They still didn't know what had caused the fire, but it wouldn't surprise him if they never found out. There were so many things which could start a barn fire, not the least of which being one of the hands lighting up a cigar on their break and disposing of it improperly.

The image of Paige's terrified face as Riley's dream escalated meant he never really went to sleep after that. He'd rushed in to try and save her the same way he'd done for Rue, but this time he'd been unsuccessful. Just before he'd jolted awake, a beam from above them came crashing down and made enough of a mess to keep him from being able to get to her.

Of course, then the image transformed from Paige to images aboard the *Sonia*. Those images haunted his dreams anyway, but he'd grown somewhat used to the poor night's sleep by this point.

Pastor Olsen stepped out onto the back porch of the church, softly nudging the blocks which kept the door open so they could get started. "You coming inside, Riley? Or are you planning to just sit outside and listen?" He glanced around and took a deep breath in the cool morning air of September. "Can't say I blame you."

"No, Pastor, I'm coming. I just needed a few minutes before going in." Riley climbed the steps and moved the block from the other door just as Pastor Olsen clapped a hand on his shoulder.

"How are you feeling?"

Riley held up his bandaged hand, a bit of frustration welling in him at the thought of how long he'd be inhibited at work. "Could've been much worse, so I'm thankful."

He followed Pastor Olsen inside and took a seat in the pew next to Lizzie, Paul, and their children. Coralee scrambled from her father's lap to come sit with Riley, but Timothy remained content in his mother's arms. He did flash a toothy grin his way, and Riley's heart melted a little in gratitude for getting to have a relationship with these children. This family was the only family he had left, and the children healed his heart in a way he could never have expected when he left Boston.

"It's my Cora-bug," he said with a tight hug and tweak of the three-year-old's braid. "You look mighty pretty this morning in your blue dress."

"Fank you, Uncle Riley! Mama made it, and she said I have to be very careful not to get it dirty."

Her eyes took on a serious hue, and Riley heard his sister snort from beside him. "We'll see how that goes."

With a tweak to Timothy's nose, the one and a half year old let out a giggle which had everyone in the pews around them turning towards them with wide grins. His attention back to Coralee, Riley nodded with mock seriousness. "I have no doubt you can do it, Bug."

Satisfied for the moment, Coralee settled back against Riley as Pastor Olsen took his place at the podium. A few pews in front of them on the other side of the church, Riley spotted Paige staring at him with something between surprise and warmth. He smiled at her and tipped his chin forward in greeting, but her cheeks flushed as she realized she'd been caught staring. That was probably better anyway, as one of the woman's smiles was bound to set him back in his determination to stay away from her.

"Good morning folks," Pastor Olsen said with a grin. "First, a little housekeeping regarding the fire at the Pratt ranch yesterday. We are all so thankful no one was hurt, but they did lose their barn entirely. Thankfully, Samuel and his hands were able to fashion a lean-to shelter last night that'll work for the time being, but with all of his seasonal help having moved on, I asked him if a barn raising might be helpful. He said it would, and we've got a plan to head out there Friday morning, work all day, and have a little social that evening. You're welcome to come to any or all of it if you can."

Barn raisings were something Riley had been wholly unfamiliar with as he moved from Boston a few years before, but they were relatively common in these parts. Usually, the whole family would go, and the children would play while the women visited and made sure everyone had plenty to eat, and the men did the building. Afterwards, somebody would get out a fiddle, and there would be a dance of sorts.

Riley had always enjoyed the food, but the dance portion never held much allure for him. That was, until he caught himself imagining what it would be like to take a pretty girl with big blue eyes for a spin around the dance floor.

As though she could read his mind, Lizzie elbowed him in the side and grinned. "Might want to wipe the drool off your chin," she whispered. "She might catch you staring."

Narrowing his eyes at his sister, Riley did indeed wipe his chin only to find it bone dry. "Funny, sis."

Based on the light shake of her shoulders, it was clear Lizzie thought so, and Riley fought to keep his mind on the sermon Pastor Harold had just started. It was a shame he'd be retiring and moving to Texas within the next few weeks, as Riley had learned more under his teaching than his entire time in the large and ornate churches of Boston. Still, he couldn't begrudge the man's desire to slow down, especially after the health scare he had the month before.

After church, Riley followed Lizzie and her family out the back door, though Coralee had shifted herself into a piggyback ride and begged him to go faster.

"Patience Cora-bug. I can't push through people just because you want to play horsey." It was her favorite game, and Riley loved to oblige her in it.

Coralee squealed with glee. "Giddy up! Let's go, horsey!"

Once he made it through the door, Riley took off at a run towards the field to the east of the church. He alternated between a gallop and a jog, but his niece's delight was worth it. Just about the time he'd tired himself out, he caught sight of something that bathed his joy from a moment before in a sea of red.

At the side of the church house, Donnie had cornered Paige and was clearly trying to sweet talk her into something. Based on her expression, she wasn't buying it, but Donnie's proximity to Paige grated on Riley nonetheless.

"Hey, Bug," he said as he placed Coralee on the ground. "Do you see your Papa right there?" He pointed to Paul, as the man's large frame was likely easier to spot than Lizzie's. When she nodded, he tugged gently on a braid. "Run on over and go see him. Uncle Riley's got something he needs to take care of."

Surprisingly, she didn't protest, and her braids flew behind her as she took off towards her father. By that point though, Riley had fixed his attention to where Donnie reached out to touch Paige's cheek, only to have her step away. "I've told you twice now, Donnie. I'm not interested. Move on."

Unbridled rage bubbled in Riley's stomach as he watched Donnie step in Paige's path once more. Something in him registered Liam and Samuel also headed their way, but he'd already reached them. Without thinking, Riley clasped Donnie's shoulder and jerked him backwards so hard the man stumbled. "She told you she wasn't interested."

His tone was somewhere between a growl and a groan, but he couldn't seem to get a handle on his anger at Donnie's complete disregard for Paige's rebuff. He'd seen enough men treating women like property at the shipyard in Boston, and he wasn't about to stand by and watch it happen to Paige.

Donnie stepped toward him, fist raised as Paige shouted in the background. As he swung, Riley ducked just in time to hear Donnie's fist make contact with flesh and a decidedly feminine squeak.

"Paige," Liam shouted as he and Samuel finally reached them. "Are you okay?"

Understanding sunk into Riley like a burning flame, and he whirled around to see Paige holding a sleeve to her nose. Tears had already begun spilling from her eyes, but there was no blood he could see. "I'm fine," she said in a nasally tone. "He just barely clipped me."

Rage and regret warred within Riley as he spun back towards Donnie. Before he could take a step and tackle the man to the ground for hurting Paige, a hand landed on his shoulder with more force than he'd have thought possible from her small frame.

"No," Paige said adamantly as fire raged behind her still watery eyes. "You're done. I'll not have two men fighting over me on my first Sunday in town, particularly when I'm not with either of you."

With that, Paige turned on her heel and stalked off towards where Kate, Mara, and Doctor Collins rushed toward her. There still wasn't any blood, so hopefully she wouldn't bruise too badly. Already, Liam had stepped between him and Donnie. "Give me one reason I shouldn't slap the cuffs on you right now, Gray."

"Because he's the one who started it, *Sheriff.*" He spat the last word as though it meant nothing. "Didn't you see him try to toss me to the ground?"

Liam narrowed his eyes, voice low and threatening. "What I saw was Riley stepping in when you tried to intimidate Paige into talking to you. I'm giving you a warning this time, but if I hear of you bothering her one more time, you'll be spending the night in jail."

Despite his clear efforts to look nonchalant, Donnie seethed just below the surface and a manner that was evident to anybody watching. "You can't have both sisters, Pratt. That's not how it works."

The only thing keeping Riley from planting his own fist into Donnie's nose at the insinuation was he couldn't look out for Paige at all if he ended up in jail too.

Rather than dignify the man's word with a response, Liam just shook his head and raised an eyebrow in Donnie's direction before walking back towards the women and Doctor Collins. Thankfully, Donnie didn't stick around, and by the time Riley realized he's tucked tail and ran, he was a few hundred yards away.

Had he done the right thing? Maybe not. But if pressed, he knew there was nothing in the world to keep him from doing the exact same thing if the situation happened again. Paige could be angry and embarrassed if she wanted. He'd hesitated one minute too long before, and a woman ended up dead. It wouldn't happen again, not if he had anything to say about it.

Chapter Five

Kate smoothed back fly away hair from Paige's face, her expression full of concern and confusion. "What in the world just happened?"

To be honest, the last thing Paige wanted to do was rehash the situation with Donnie and Riley, but these were her friends, her sisters - Mara especially. "Donnie has decided I'm a conquest he's interested in pursuing, and Riley has decided I'm a responsibility that needs protecting." Her words might be harsh, but it was the truth. She'd spent her entire life feeling like someone else's responsibility, and the idea Riley would only defend her because he felt guilty grated on her.

Maybe she was being unfair to Riley, but the whole situation had been unnecessarily escalated by his interference. She couldn't help but feel a little embarrassed. Mara, uncharacteristically quiet since she approached the group, spoke up then. "What did you expect Riley to do? Liam had already spotted the two of you and headed your way, mostly so I didn't do it myself. Riley hasn't handled every piece of this situation perfectly, but he did nothing wrong here."

Annoyance flooded Paige's body at her sister's words, but mostly because she knew Mara was right. Turning to face Riley, Liam, and Samuel where they stared off after Donnie Gray weakened her ire a little. Riley flexed his burned hand, massaging it through the bandages, and she realized it was the same hand he'd used to push Donnie away from her.

Had he injured himself further on her behalf? Any last remaining desire to tell him to mind his own business faded away as she spotted the battle raging on his face. He looked her way, his amber eyes full of concern and uncertainty. She hadn't realized she'd begun walking his direction until she reached the small group of men and came to a stop beside the man who could've been her husband by then.

"Can we talk for a moment?"

His eyes widened, but he nodded all the same. The tall oak at the back of the church yard seemed as good a place as any, and the soft brush of Riley's boots on the grass told her he was only a few steps behind her. A soft breeze rustled across the fields which surrounded the church on three sides, and the mountains stood guard over the valleys below.

They reached the tree, and Paige broke the silence. "I have to admit, I'm looking forward to winter here. I've only ever seen a light dusting of snow in New Orleans, but my father used to read us a book every Christmas where the family takes a sleigh into town over the snowy roads." She shrugged, unsure why she was telling him this. "It always seemed so romantic to me, though I'll probably eat my words once I slip on a patch of ice and fall flat on my face."

He chuckled, the deep, throaty sound comforting despite the embarrassment from the situation with Donnie. "You might, but I've had my fair share of frustration with the winters here and still prefer it to Boston. We have snow there too, but the open space out here makes everything look a little mystical. The pure white reminds a body what it means to be forgiven, I guess."

Did he mean for stepping in with Donnie? The pain in his eyes told her he didn't, but there was still so much she didn't know about the man before her. "I didn't bring you over here to yell at you, by the way."

"Well that's a relief, because I'm not even the least bit sorry for stepping in." He shoved his hands in his pockets, the truth in his words clear. "I stood by once when I knew better and an innocent woman wound up paying the price. I know you have issues with feeling like a burden, but I vowed to myself as long as I had breath, I'd stand up for what's right."

Paige had the suspicion he wouldn't explain further even if she asked, so she focused on the subject at hand. "Mara told me Donnie's got a history of going after women who aren't his to chase, so I assume he'll get bored soon. Still, I appreciate your help." It pricked her pride, but she had to admit having someone in her corner felt nice.

Riley's eyes darkened, and he resumed studying the landscape before them. "If he or anyone else gives you trouble, I want you to come to me or Liam or Paul. I'd prefer to know about it, but I know that may be too tall of a request. I just can't stand the idea of you here in town alone." His gaze moved from the mountains in the distance to his bandaged hand, and she wished so badly to be able to read his thoughts.

"I'm not really alone here," she reminded him. "I'm staying with the Olsens, and I work with Stew. Mara and Liam are here too, and you know how overprotective my sister is."

"I do, but you're only with the Olsens for a few weeks until the new pastor comes into town. No matter what, I just want you to be careful." The tension in his shoulders broke her heart a little.

His concern, while not wholly necessary, did feel the tiniest bit nice. As though her hand had its own brain, she placed it on his arm and tried to ignore how right it felt. "I don't know what kind of past you're running from, Riley, but I'm here if you ever need to talk."

At that moment, the veil slapped back down over his eyes as though she'd never caught a glimpse at all. "Well, I'd better get back to the ranch. You take care of yourself, alright?"

The abrupt shift might have given her a crick in her neck if she hadn't half expected it the moment she brought up his past. Somehow, despite barely knowing the man, she found his cues easy to read. It was as though a shadow closed over his expression, shutting him off from the world around him - or at least from her.

Why she cared, she couldn't have said, but somewhere between his panicked assurances he'd not been the one to send off for a bride and that moment underneath the old oak, she had indeed grown to care. The only question was whether it would fade with time or she'd be forced to see him week after week as he moved on with his life.

Still, all she could do was trust the Lord had a plan greater than hers. No matter how alone she might have felt in her life, He'd never abandoned her. Even now, in the midst of everything else going on, she was surrounded by people who cared about her. The Olsens had been so incredibly kind, Paul and Lizzie checked in on her regularly, and Liam and Mara were barely a stone's throw away. No, she wasn't alone, and any feelings she developed for Riley would just have to be given to the Lord the same way anything else in her life would.

If Riley could've somehow managed to pull his booted foot all the way up to kick himself in the behind, he would. As it was, he was hindered by the fact he'd never been all that flexible and he was currently atop Winchester, the ten-year-old stallion he'd purchased with his first few months of ranch hand money years before.

The conversation with Paige had started out well enough, but the way he'd tucked tail and run once she mentioned his past was almost as cowardly as Donnie do-ing the same. Still, the fact he'd even mentioned Alice at all was more than he'd told anyone else. Not a day went by he didn't ache for Alice's children, and it was only in the last year he'd stopped sending money back east to them as her youngest daughter had gotten married.

Still, they didn't have their mother, and that fact would never change. Taking him under her wing at a time when he'd never felt more alone, Alice had been like a mother to him when his own had passed and Lizzie moved to Col-orado with Paul. Her graying hair and small wrinkles only served to make her even more captivating to him, her warm smile and spirit of hospitality something sixteen-year-old Riley had needed more than he'd needed his next breath.

Tears pricked the backs of his eyes, but the telltale thump of cantering horse hooves behind him had him swallowing them down. He had no doubt he'd turn to find at least one of the Pratt brothers following him, and it wouldn't surprise him if they'd both come along.

As it turned out, it was indeed both of them and they each slowed their mounts to a walk once they reached him. Neither spoke for a second, but Liam unsurprisingly was the one to break the silence. "So, you gonna tell us what happened between the two of you, or am I gonna have to start making up stories in my head?"

"Don't test him," Samuel grumbled from the other side of Riley. "He'll do it, and then he'll spread rumors all over town."

Liam chuckled, a self satisfied smirk on his face. "And sometimes, fifteen years later, they still believe the reason you went home from school early was because you didn't make it to the outhouse in time and not that you came down with chicken pox."

The two of them bickered good-naturedly for another minute or so, but Riley saw right through it. "Are you two done trying to wear me down, or did you still have more grievances to air out?"

"Depends," Liam replied. "You ready to tell us what happened?"

"You saw as much of what happened with Donnie as I did, but she wasn't mad like I'd have expected." Honestly, it might've been better if she had been, because then he probably wouldn't have spouted off about his past like he had. "She thanked me, actually."

With a whistle, Samuel nodded. "That's a first from these New Orleans gals, at least before you earn their trust. Either Kate and Mara talked to her, or she's a little less stubborn than the two of them."

"It's the first one," Liam said. "I caught Mara on the way out, and she gave me the run down. Plus, I think Donnie might have spooked her more than she let on, especially after what happened at the restaurant."

The haze of red that had taken over when Riley saw Donnie grab Paige threatened the corners of his vision once more. "What happened at the restaurant?"

"Down boy. Stew handled it, and he banned Donnie from ever coming back. I am getting tired of his trying to charm other men's brides though. If he's that lonely, why wouldn't he send for one himself?"

Riley raised an eyebrow and studied Liam. "You'd wish him on any woman?"

"Of course not, I'd warn her the second she got to town, but you'd think he'd at least try." Liam paused, his lips pursed like it did when he was thinking through a crime. "You don't think he's the one who sent off on your behalf, do you?"

With a snort, Samuel leaned forward and looked past Riley to his brother. "For what purpose? Do we think Donnie's turned into a matchmaker now? He never did bother Kate, but she mostly stayed out at the ranch when she arrived." Riley didn't miss the way the cowboy's fists tightened on his reins, and he had no doubt exactly how it would pan out if Donnie ever tried.

"No, but it wasn't that far-fetched to assume they wouldn't actually go through with it." Liam sent a pointed look in Riley's direction. "Get a girl here, then she realizes she's alone with no groom. The wrench in his plan was it was actually my wife's sister, and she's very much not alone after all." He shrugged. "The only thing I can't figure out is motive. Why not just send off for a bride himself?"

The possibility rolled over in Riley's mind a few times, but for some reason his gut told him that wasn't it. Donnie was a pest, but was he even smart enough to think up something like that? "I guess we may never know, but I plan to have a talk with Donnie about leaving her alone from now on."

"Why don't you let me handle that?" Liam spoke then with all the calm confidence of a seasoned lawman. "I'd rather not have to toss you in a cell, and there's no way a conversation between you and Donnie doesn't come to blows right now." Riley opened his mouth to argue, but Liam cut him off. "Hey, trust me, I don't begrudge anyone the desire to plant a fist in his smug little face, but I don't think you'd keep your head. At least let me try first. If I can't get him to back off, you're welcome to get yourself thrown in the slammer."

"You know," Samuel spoke up. "You could just marry Paige and save everyone a whole lot of trouble. You clearly like her, and she came out here planning on a marriage of convenience anyway."

"I actually already told her I would, but she turned me down. Besides, I don't even have a place to bring a bride home to."

Samuel shook his head, something between compassion and amusement clear in his expression. "I already told you I'd deed you a small plot of land and help you build a cabin. You two would be welcome to stay with us until it was ready. It's not like we don't have the room."

"I think you're missing the important part," Liam said. "He said he already asked her, and she said no."

"No, he told her he would. That's different, especially for a woman who came out here feeling like a burden to folks. If I were a betting man, I'd also bet my hat he said something along the lines of her being his responsibility." Samuel pinned Riley with a knowing look. "That right?"

Both men took Riley's silence as confirmation, because both let out a "tsk tsk."

"Just think about it," Samuel said as he nudged Roscoe into a faster gait. "Not from a standpoint of responsibility, but of something she might actually accept." He took off towards the ranch, leaving both of them in the dust.

Just then, Riley realized neither of their wives were anywhere to be seen. "Where are Kate and Mara?"

"Spending the afternoon in town with Paige. We're going back to get them after dinner." A wide grin stretched over Liam's face. "So you get us all to yourself." With that, he nudged his own mount into a canter and headed toward the ranch as well.

The dust rose up behind both of them in a cloud which seemed to taunt Riley with exactly how much more well meaning meddling waited for him at the ranch. Unfortunately, ranch work never stopped, and he had work he needed to do. So, the Pratt brothers it was. "Good for me," he grumbled with a sigh. "Exactly what I needed."

Chapter Six

Paige flipped the chicken sizzling in the restaurant's heavy iron pan, content at the golden brown crust which had formed during its time in the heat. "Atta girl," she told the food before her without the slightest bit of self consciousness at talking to food. "Now, let's check on your friends."

As though in a bit of a trance, Paige gave the rest of the chicken the same treatment as the lunch rush approached. Stew had given her more and more responsibility in the kitchen, and it didn't hurt that every single one of his customers told him he'd better do so. She sprinkled a little more salt onto the chicken and let the other side crisp and turned her attention to the bread which had just finished up in the oven, the smell of perfectly baked loaves signaling it was time to remove them.

As she did, she took a moment to thank the Lord she'd landed a job here doing the thing she loved. Taking food from raw ingredients to something delicious and nourishing never failed to lift her spirits and put things to rights. Cooking was part art, part science, and losing herself in the creation of it over the last week had given her time to form perspective over what had happened at church on Sunday.

Riley was a good man, and there was a great deal no one knew about him, but she had to let go of the dream of stepping off the train to the smiling face of her groom. In the weeks since she'd first boarded the train, she'd conjured up an image of a love like the one her sister found with a handsome cowboy who unfortunately didn't hold a candle to Riley's actual looks.

Flipping the loaf pans to release the bread, she inhaled its fresh scent. There was no way she could've developed actual feelings for Riley in as little time as she'd known him, so it had to be down to the dream she'd become attached to. At least, she hoped it was.

The rest of her shift passed quickly, her aching lower back the only indication how long she'd been working that day. By the time Stew came back and told her she could head on home to the Olsens, she could barely believe it.

Still, stepping out into the fading sunlight felt good, and she basked in it for a moment before heading toward the mercantile for a few things she needed.

A familiar voice cut through her senses, its friendly baritone welcome. "Mara does the same thing," Liam said fondly as he approached from the street. "She'll stand in the sun, close her eyes, and just breathe. Must be a sister thing."

Paige grinned, her own unrealized dream with Riley not at all dampening the happiness she felt for her sister and her groom. "What can I say? The Brown girls love a little sunshine."

"That they do. Are you headed home?" Liam gestured towards the parsonage in the distance, visible from the restaurant if one squinted their eyes. "I'd be happy to walk you."

"I'm actually headed to the mercantile to pick up a few things, but I imagine Mara will be getting off soon if you'd like to come with me." The way his whole face brightened at the idea of seeing his wife had Paige grinning from ear to ear. "I'll take that as a yes."

Just as they reached the mercantile, Paige spotted the train pulling out of the makeshift depot in the distance. It was hard to believe only a few weeks ago she'd been stepping off the train to the same view of the mountains and sky. A short man in an expensive looking suit moved with purpose away from the platform, checking something on a paper as he went. He held a satchel and his jet black hair and mustache were punctuated by a pair of glasses and a slightly crooked nose.

He held his hand in the air to flag them down, and Liam motioned for her to stay where she was. "How can I help you, sir?"

The suited man came to an abrupt stop in front of Liam and spoke with as much energy as he'd walked. He eyed Liam's badge with satisfaction and held out his hand. "Aah, perfect. Nice to meet you, Sheriff. I'm Horace Potts, U.S. Attorney in Boston. Would you happen to know where I might find Mr. Riley Hart?"

As though of their own accord, Paige's feet began to move in the mens' direction. "What do you want with Riley?" Possibilities flooded her mind, and she had the inexplicable urge to ride out to the ranch and warn him. Too bad she couldn't ride a horse to save her life, never having had the chance in New Orleans.

Liam shook the man's hand and spoke with an annoyingly calm voice. "May I ask what it's regarding?"

Mr. Potts narrowed his eyes at Liam for a moment as his eyes darted between the two of them. Apparently, deciding they weren't a threat, he sighed and reached into the outer pocket of his satchel. Handing Liam the official looking document, Paige could only make out the words at the top before Liam angled it away from her. The words splashed across the top, "SUMMONS TO APPEAR," sent her gut roiling almost as much as the official U.S. Attorney General's insignia in the corner.

What did that mean? Was Riley in trouble? Had he left Boston due to a crime he'd committed? He said something about a woman getting hurt, but surely he hadn't hurt anyone. The Riley she thought she knew never would, but did she really know him at all?

Liam nodded towards Mr. Potts and folded the paper before handing it back. "I'll take you to Riley." Addressing Paige now, gone was the good-natured face of her brother-in-law and in place was the officially impartial one of a lawman. "Go on to the mercantile without me, and let Mara know I'll be a little late tonight."

His words left no room for argument, nor did his tone, and Paige could do nothing but nod and stare after the two men as they started off down the street towards the livery. If she'd been her sister, she might've run off after them and demanded answers, but then she'd have regretted it later.

No, she'd have to wait, and in the meantime she'd tell no one what happened. Lizzie was Riley's sister, and worrying her unnecessarily seemed cruel. Still, U.S. Attorneys didn't just just show up in tiny towns in Colorado for anything less than important cases.

The realization the sun had begun its slow descent over the mountains reminded her of the time, and she'd better get to the mercantile if she wanted to arrive before closing time. Mara would know something preoccupied her, but she'd just have to do her best to keep it from being obvious. She owed Riley that much for the kindness he'd shown her - the right to share the details as he pleased.

Riley sat back in one of Samuel and Kate's kitchen chairs, running a hand over his face. "I was afraid this would happen." Liam and Mr. Potts watched him as he took in the news. Liam's expression showed compassion and concern, while Mr. Potts's eyes blazed with the fire of a prosecutor intent on bringing the bad guys to justice. Knowing that bolstered his courage, and he nodded resolutely. "What do you need from me, Mr. Potts?"

"First, I come with apologies on behalf of the Boston Police Department. They failed you, and they failed Mrs. McKinley."

Alice. The innocent woman with three children who'd died as a result of the detective's lack of urgency regarding Riley's tip and his own failure to escalate the situation. "I hope they extended the same apology to Alice's family, and that detective is no longer in their employ." Detective Stallings had basically patted seventeen-year-old Riley on the head and sent him on his way, effectively signing Alice's death certificate.

"They did, but of course that will never bring their mother back." Spinning the summons on the table to where it faced Riley, Mr. Potts's face remained respectfully grave. "We can't bring Mrs. McKinley back, but you can help ensure those responsible for her death are held accountable. Your full cooperation with our investigation is key."

Memories assailed Riley from that day aboard the *Sonia*, and his fingers absently went to the spot on his abdomen where he'd forever carry a physical reminder to go with them. As if he'd ever forget. "What's the likelihood of Randolph and his men going to prison? He's got more money than he could ever spend, and it's my word against his. How do I know he's not going to just wiggle out of the charges like he has before?"

"Fair question," Potts said. "This is the first time he's been federally charged, and the only way he'll get me off his case is to take out a hit on me." He shrugged, clearly resigned to the fact it was a good possibility. "I have no family left, Mr. Hart. I've been more or less married to my job for three decades, and I have nothing I'm not willing to lose in the pursuit of justice. Mrs. McKinley isn't the only person who's lost their life to his carelessness, but I'm committed to making her one of the last."

Studying the set of the man's jaw, the honesty in his eyes, Riley couldn't help but trust him. "Speaking of hits, how can I ensure the people I care about are safe? I do have things to lose, sir." Images of Lizzie, Paul, and their children flashed through his mind, as did friends who'd become more like family in the years he'd been in Mud Lake. Lastly, in a moment that shouldn't have surprised him, Paige's face appeared as well. "How can I ensure they're protected?"

He'd been summoned, so there was little choice in his court appearance, but Riley knew what Mr. Potts was really asking. Would he be completely honest, and would he share every bit of the events he'd tried to report to Detective Stallings back in Boston? Had his warnings been heeded, or had he gone over the man's head, Alice would still be alive.

Mr. Potts shifted his focus to Liam, and Riley could see the wheels turning in his friend's mind. "I can bring in a protective detail from Boston, but I'm afraid that would cause more harm than good with the attention it would draw. Do you have any contacts with the U.S. Marshals in Denver?"

"I do, and we've worked together in the past. I'll take care of contacting them as soon as we get back into town, but I'm still unclear on exactly what happened in Boston. I know some of the information might be privileged, but I don't like facing down an enemy I don't understand. Anything you can give me would be much appreciated."

"Mr. Hart," Potts said as he shut his briefcase, "that's up to you."

He was right, and it was time Liam knew what had driven him from Boston at eighteen years old. "When I was sixteen, after Lizzie left to marry Paul, I got a job with Randolph Shipping..."

Chapter Seven

Paige watched the gorgeous black and white Appaloosa bob his head with a wild look in his eyes as she stood at the edge of the Pratt ranch corral. "Oh Kate, he's beautiful." He was clearly underweight, but time at the ranch would hopefully fix that quickly.

She'd come out with Mara that morning to spend some time with Kate, but the ranch had just received a new training client for Joshua. Apparently, the owner had purchased the horse without laying eyes on the thing, and it was as buck wild as buck wild could be. That's what Joshua said anyway, but other than the darting of his eyes and occasional pawing the ground, he seemed relatively calm.

"I know," Kate said fondly. "I feel so bad for him having to stay in this corral until Joshua can introduce him to the other horses and see how he does." She held out a hand, carrot in her palm, and clicked her tongue softly. "Come on over if you want it, Dakota."

He bobbed his black and white spotted head but didn't make a move to approach the edge of the corral. From her other side, Paige could sense her sister's sadness even before she heard the tell tale sniffle. Of course, Mara would relate to the horse who'd been treated so unfairly, her heart broken at the idea of him in any sort of cage. They wouldn't leave him there long, according to Kate, but they needed to watch him for disease before they could allow him near the other horses. Mara sniffed again, clutching the fence posts with white knuckles. "Can't you just let him go?"

"He's not our horse, but no. The man who bought him didn't realize how malnourished he was, and he's got some sort of infection on his front leg Joshua says needs to be treated."

With that, Mara backed away from the corral fence, clearly unable to see the animal denied his freedom anymore. "I understand, but I can't watch him behind the fence anymore. Do you mind if I go take a walk in your garden?"

"Not at all. In fact, I'll come with you." Kate turned to Paige, gesturing towards the bounty of a garden behind their farmhouse. "Want to come, Paige?" She tossed the carrot into the middle of the corral for Dakota, the horse still keeping his distance.

Unafflicted with the same hatred of any sort of cage or fence as her sister, Paige shook her head. "No, I'd like to watch him for a little longer if that's all right. I'll see if I can get him to eat a carrot from my hand so I can brag he likes me better." She winked at Kate, who chuckled as she waved and followed Mara. It wasn't Paige was heartless, she felt bad for Dakota too. She just felt the animal was in the best place for him at the moment and held great hope for his rehabilitation in the capable hands of the Pratt ranch wrangler. According to Mara and Kate, they treated everyone well, from the humans who worked for them to the animals they cared for.

Paige leaned down to pull another carrot from the bucket at her feet, holding it out the way she'd seen Kate do. Paige had always loved horses despite never having ridden one and knowing nothing about them. They always seemed like gentle giants in the streets of New Orleans, but the few times she'd approached to pet one, she'd been shooed away by store owners due to her street urchin designation.

"Come on, boy. I won't hurt you." Dakota's ears pricked forward, and he took a single step towards her. He pawed the ground a few more times but gobbled the carrot Kate had tossed when he reached it. "That's it. Don't you want another one?"

After what felt like ten more minutes of him taking a step or two forward only to back up again, Dakota finally got close enough to take the carrot from Paige's hand. Joshua had managed to get a bridle on him, but nothing else. It was a simple design, one that appeared to be less trouble to get on and off, but she didn't really know.

"Want one more? I don't want to feed you too much without asking, but carrots are healthy, right?" Plus, goodness knew he needed to fatten up a little. She picked a small one, just in case too much might upset his stomach, and held it up once more. He moved a little quicker this time, gobbling the carrot with as much gusto as he had the other two. As he pulled back, however, the makeshift bridle got stuck on one of the fence posts, and Dakota's panic at the realization had him yanking and wedging it further down.

"Uh oh," Paige said as she pulled at the rope. "Let me see if I can get you free, boy." Try as she might, the rope wouldn't budge with the way he continued to pull back. Sweat started to shimmer on his coat, and his eyes and nostrils widened. "No, no," she said as softly as she could as her fingers tried to pull the rope free. "If you'll just relax a little, this will be much easier."

In the current position, she had no leverage to move Dakota even an inch forward to free the rope, and the way he was pulling it was likely he'd hurt himself. If only she could approach the rope from the other direction, but that would require her entering the corral. That would mean disobeying Samuel's one instruction regarding the green broke animal.

Still, there was no one else around, and Kate and Mara would probably insist on firing a shot in the air to summon one of the men. That would only terrify Dakota further, and he might well hurt himself. The way he continued to yank, the rope no doubt cutting into his skin, she refused to think too much about her decision. "All right, calm down. I'm coming."

Balling her skirt up as modestly as she could despite the fact no one was around, Paige climbed to the first rung of the corral fence before swinging herself over the rest of the way. Her feet landed with a soft thud on the grass covered ground, and she approached Dakota slowly from the side. "I'm here to help, and then I'll get right back out."

As gently as she could, she pulled Dakota's head forward just enough to wrench the bridle rope free from the fence post. Knowing it would be foolish to stay inside one minute longer than she had to, Paige took a step toward the fence only for Dakota's head to whip around wildly and knock her off balance. Her backside hit the ground only a few feet from the stallion's powerful hooves, and he'd already moved from pawing the ground to rearing.

Fear surged in Paige's blood, and she could nearly feel her heart beating out of her chest. As she scrambled backwards, she distantly registered shouts from multiple directions. All of a sudden, just as Dakota took another step toward her and reared again, a strong arm grabbed her around the waist and yanked her up as though she weighed nothing.

She flew through the air until she hit another broad chest which quickly set her on her feet. As Liam's hands steadied her outside the corral, she spotted Riley hopping over the wooden fence after her. He didn't even pause for a moment as his feet covered the few steps between them. "Are you all right? He didn't get you, did he?"

Riley's eyes were as panicked as Dakota's had been, guilt rising as she acknowledged her role in its presence. "I'm fine. I'm sorry. It's all my fault."

The rest of the group reached them then, Samuel, Kate, Mara, Joshua, and Clarence bringing up the rear. Samuel's voice was low, angry as he spoke. "Why in the world did you go in there, Paige? Do you have any idea how dangerous that was? If Riley hadn't gotten there when he did, we might've had to shoot Dakota to save you. Not to mention, it could have been too late." His face was beet red under his beard, and the shame only increased in Paige's belly.

"Samuel," Riley said through gritted teeth. "Don't talk to her like that. She knows it was wrong." Turning his attention to her, his voice only mildly more relaxed than his boss's, Riley spoke. "What happened?"

Samuel still looked angry, but Kate's hand on his arm seemed to calm him some, while Mara's expression was still one of pure panic. "I gave him a carrot, and he ate it out of my hand." Joshua's brows rose at that, but she continued. "He got his bridle stuck on that notch in the fence, and he kept yanking it so hard I was afraid he'd hurt himself. I knew if I could just get his head forward a little, I could pull it free. I shouldn't have done it."

Voice still low, Samuel spoke a little more calmly. "Why didn't you fire off a shot?"

"I was afraid it would scare him, and he'd hurt himself," she said quietly.

Riley placed two gentle hands on her arms. "So you thought you'd sacrifice yourself to keep him from hurting himself?" He blew out a hard breath and shut his eyes. "I'm assuming you know better than to ever do that again?"

Heart finally slowing enough to take a good breath, she nodded. "I do."

"Good."

Later that day, Riley returned from the field to find Paige sitting alone in the makeshift barn they'd fashioned out of a lean-to and some scrap lumber until the barn raising later that weekend. The tear tracks on her face broke his heart a little, but he knew they were more from embarrassment and regret than anything else. When he'd seen her hit the ground in the corral, it was as though nothing in the world could have kept him from her in that moment. He'd run faster than he'd have ever guessed possible and all but flew over the fence to reach her.

It was a good thing Liam had been barely a step behind him, or she'd have hit the ground outside the corral with much more force than she did inside. Still, it would've been drastically preferable to getting trampled by a horse. Even Joshua had been surprised Dakota had allowed her to feed him from her hand, but the foolishness of her choice to enter the corral remained.

She knew that, though, as was evidenced by the slight shake of her shoulders as she sat on a square hay bale in the barn all by herself. She buried her face in her hands, and just like earlier, Riley was irresistibly pulled towards her. "Hey now, what's this about?"

Her head popped up, but she didn't bother to try and hide her tears. "Riley."

His name sounded good on her lips, and he found himself wishing he could hear it more. Slowly, not unlike how he might approach a green broke filly, Riley moved toward her. "It's okay. Samuel's over it, and he feels bad for how he spoke to you."

"He shouldn't. It was all my fault. I tried to fix it myself and I just..." She sniffed again, and he got the distinct impression the tears were about far more than just the scene with Dakota.

Helpless to his better judgment, Riley wrapped his arm around Paige and tugged her into his side. She hesitated for only a moment before surrendering and resting her head on his shoulder. "You made a mistake, Paige. No one got hurt, and Dakota's just fine. Don't be so hard on yourself.

Forgive yourself, or it'll eat at you." If anyone knew that, he did.

She was quiet for a moment before pulling up to angle her head toward him. "Why do I get the feeling that's advice you probably need to take yourself?" His sharp intake of breath was the only sound he made, but she narrowed her eyes slightly. "I met Mr. Potts in town the other day."

Leaving the words hanging, he took them for what they were. It was his decision to explain or not, and the options warred within him. He'd not known her long, but he'd not been able to shake thoughts of her from that first day in town. Something like an invisible thread kept drawing them together, and the desire for her to know every piece of him won out. "I've been summoned to Boston to testify in a trial against my old boss."

"What happened?" Her words were gentle, her cheeks still slightly pink from her earlier tears.

Where did he start? "Has anyone told you our parents died right before Lizzie moved out here with Paul?"

She shook her head. "I'm so sorry, Riley."

"Thank you. Knowing they're with Jesus is the only way either of us were able to move forward. Lizzie begged me to come to Mud Lake with them, but I was sixteen years old and wanted to make my own way."

Paige scoffed a little, pursing her lips as she did. "I know how that feels."

"I got a job with Randolph Shipping, one of the largest shipping corporations on the east coast. Augustus Randolph was known around town for cutting corners to save money, but he always paid inspectors to look the other way. It never really affected me until I moved out of the shipyard aboard the *Sonia*. I worked in the boiler room. It was backbreaking work, but it paid for the room I rented at the boarding house and the food I needed. My goal was to work my way up and make something of myself in the shipping industry, but all that went down the drain when I blew the whistle on some safety violations I reported."

It had started out innocuous enough, a broken valve here, a faulty hose there, but when his reports to superiors went unaddressed, he finally went to the police. A close call with one of his coworkers was what finally drove him to it, but the fear and anger had been compounding for months.

"I'd grown close to another family in the boarding house. They had children a few years younger than me, and the mother basically treated me like one of her own. She made sure I packed a lunch everyday, but one day I forgot." Memories of Alice scolding him for being too thin whirled in his memory, as did her bringing lunch down to the shipyard when he forgot. "Alice McKinley was good as gold. She mothered everyone around her, and her husband had worked for Randolph as well before he passed away. She took a job across the street from the shipyard as a laundress, so if I ever left the boarding house without enough food, she'd take it upon herself to bring me something."

"She sounds lovely," Paige said softly. His arm was still wrapped around her, but he couldn't bring himself to remove it.

"She was." The realization in Paige's eyes at his use of the past tense was clear, and he continued. "The day she died, I was aboard the *Sonia* down in the boiler room. I'd told her never to board that ship to bring me food, but it was mostly so she didn't get bothered by the other men. She didn't listen, of course, and right around noon that day, I heard her voice calling my name from the stairs."

He'd been equal parts appreciative and annoyed she'd put herself at risk that way, but his stomach had been growling for the past hour. "I went to meet her. Before I could get there, one of the boilers close to the stairs exploded."

Paige gasped, her eyes misting as she brought her hand to her mouth. "Oh Riley." Her words sounded a little breathy, but he continued nonetheless. It was a little like lancing a wound. Once he'd started sharing, it all had to come out.

"I tried to get to her," he choked as the flashes of fire and terrified boiler men remained branded into his brain forever. "But it was too late." His hand went absently to his side as it often did when he thought back to that day. Going back to the boarding house and telling her children had been the worst moment of his entire life. Her oldest was his age, and he'd taken on the lion's share of supporting the rest of the family, but Riley had sent money to help for years. "Once the dust settled, my grief gave way to anger, and I became focused on someone paying for the crime. It was evident pretty quickly a faulty valve was the culprit for the explosion, and it was purely preventable. Someone had to pay."

He hadn't particularly cared who it was at the time, as both his supervisors and the police department had failed them all. Not only had Alice died that day, but a handful of other Randolph Shipping employees had lost their lives as well. He looked down at Paige, straining to see any judgment in her eyes and wondering if it would be the nail in the coffin of any future for them. Instead, he found only compassion, her lip trembling while she firmly held his gaze.

"It wasn't your fault," she said so softly he barely heard her. "I can see it plain on your face you blame yourself, but you tried to report the faulty equipment. Did you get the justice you were hoping for?"

A scoff with no mirth escaped him, and he shook his head. "No. I got run out of Boston before I got a chance, and it took two more explosions aboard Randolph ships for anyone to start getting suspicious."

"Is that why Mr. Potts is here now? Are they trying?" She placed her hand in his uninjured one, the contrast of her soft and smooth hands protected in the kitchen with his work worn ones was stark, but the contact felt right.

"They are, and I've been called to testify."

Her hand tightened, and he realized just how close her lips were to his. Were they as soft as her hands? Would she push him away? He was no fool, and Paige hadn't made a secret of her attraction to him. He'd not told anyone else on earth as much about Boston as he had Paige. Even Liam and Mr. Potts likely didn't realize Alice was like a second mother to him. Lancing the wound, the one that had eaten away at him for years, felt good. Hearing her absolve him of blame, even if he didn't believe her, felt like the first deep breath he'd taken in ages.

Riley lowered his head a fraction until his lips hovered just above hers, the only sound in the barn of her quickened breathing. She didn't pull away though, and he'd almost closed the distance between them when the sound of a cow braying in the distance jarred him from the moment.

What was he doing? All the reasons he'd not sent off for a wife originally were still true, and now he'd made himself a target for any of Randolph's men who figured out where he had gone. Entering into a relationship with her now would put a target on her back as well. As though he'd been shot, Riley jerked back and jumped to his feet. "I-I'm sorry, Paige. I've got to go."

Rather than stay and explain himself, he took the coward's way out and moved as quickly as he could out of the barn. How shortsighted could he be? Paige needed to stay far away from him for her own safety, lest Randolph's men decide to come after him.

Conviction pricked his heart to trust the Lord would take care of her, but his worry and regret shoved it back down. No, the best thing he could do was stay far away from her at least until the trial was over. Then, it would be down to whether Randolph actually served time for his crime or managed to pay his way out of it.

Chapter Eight

"Stew, I think you overpaid me." Paige counted out the money he'd handed her, certain the amount was higher than the agreed upon weekly rate. "You've given me almost double."

Her boss waved a hand in front of his face. "Nah, your food has brought so many folks in who weren't regulars before I figured I'd up your pay."

Touched by the gesture, Paige's sour mood after yesterday's almost-kiss with Riley out on the ranch lifted a little. It had embarrassed and frustrated her, but mostly she just felt silly. She'd all but asked him to kiss her with the way her face angled toward his, and there was no doubt he thought her a wanton woman for such a blatant display with a man she had only known for a few weeks.

She'd never kissed a man before, but the way Riley had shared about his past cracked something in her and combined with his protective sweetness had her acting like a silly schoolgirl. As he'd jerked back and all but ran away from her, she'd wished the old barn still stood so she could climb in the hayloft Kate told her about and hide. Thankfully, they'd left soon after, but Riley was nowhere to be seen.

Oh well, no use dwelling on misread signals and unrequited crushes. She'd been blessed with double the expected paycheck, and that meant she could go over to the mercantile and get some penny candies while chatting with Lizzie and Mara. The two of them were often busy, but perhaps they'd have a few minutes.

"Thanks Stew, I really appreciate it." Without overthinking it, Paige pulled the restaurant owner into a quick hug which he turned into an awkward pat on the back.

His stiffness only relaxed minutely once she pulled back, though there was an even deeper blush than normally adorned his cheeks. "You've done good work here, and a worker is worth their wages. I'll see you tomorrow."

Clearly dismissed, Paige smirked and headed out into the sunshine of the mid-September afternoon. As much as she loved spending more and more time in the kitchen of the restaurant, the few windows in the space meant she relished the feel of the warmth on her face. She likely smelled like a mixture of all the different foods she'd prepared that day, but Mara wouldn't care.

Mouth watering at the thought of the penny candies adorning the mercantile's back wall, Paige thought of how grateful she was that small expenses like penny candies were an easy choice after so many years of scrimping just to eat a meal or two a day. The Lord had been good to her, and she had no business dwelling on things she couldn't change.

Riley clearly wasn't interested in his not-so-intended bride, and she'd not waste any more time cringing at her actions. At least, maybe if she kept telling herself that, she could make it true.

A group of boys playing in the street brought a grin to her lips. As children, she and Mara had more or less had to force their way into baseball games with the boys at first, but it was obvious quickly that both of them could hold their own. Jarred from her memories by shouts from some of the boys, she spotted a ball flying through the air and moving in such a trajectory it might break one of the bank's windows.

The little girl who'd just wanted to play baseball over double dutch took over inside her body, and she grabbed her skirt in one hand and took off for the path of the pop fly. It felt good, just like it had when she was just a girl, and she was the only one close enough to catch it.

Hoping she didn't run into anyone, Paige jumped up on the porch outside the bank at the same time the baseball reached the same spot. Dropping the fabric of her skirt which would've hindered her running, she held out a bare hand mere feet from the window. The ball smarted in her hand, sending a jolt up the nerves of her arm, but the sense of accomplishment eclipsed it.

The group of boys had all taken off running in her direction, cheering their heads off at the knowledge they hadn't broken a window and would be safe to play another day. The tallest among them had scruffy brown hair and a rip in the knee of his pants. "Thank ya, miss. That was amazing!"

Tossing the ball back to him, Paige winked at the boy with the bat in his hand. "Can't have the game getting shut down before sunset, can we? Where's the fun in that?"

The batter, around ten if her guess was correct, blushed. "Are you new in town? I don't reckon I've seen you before."

"Sure am. My name's Paige."

One of the other boys snickered, apparently not as impressed as the rest of them. "My dad said you came as a mail-order bride for Mr. Riley out at the Pratt ranch, but he didn't want to marry you after all. He reckons it won't be long until some other fella snatches you up."

Her cheeks burned a little, but she'd lived an entire life with folks forming opinions based on half truths. "That's one interpretation of the situation," she said with a shrug. "But you might not want to believe everything you hear."

With as much feigned confidence as she could muster, Paige waved goodbye to the boys and began to move back towards the mercantile. She'd wondered what sort of reputation she'd gain in town, but a jilted bride was probably better than some of the other possibilities.

She'd almost reached the mercantile when a familiar voice which had her stifling a groan pierced her thoughts. "Well, there she is," Donnie drawled from just to her left. "If I didn't know any better, I'd think you were following me."

Could this man be any more delusional? Not even attempting to keep the chagrin from her face, Paige rolled her eyes. "Considering you've been the one to approach me each time we've met, I'd say it's the other way around. Careful, Mr. Gray, I might start to think you mean to harass me. Liam wouldn't take kindly to that, I don't think."

Eyes sparking with anger, Donnie stepped forward until he towered over her. "Don't ever threaten me with Pratt.

One, I'm not afraid of him, and two, it's him who should probably be afraid of me."

The good mood she'd been sporting a few minutes before had fully faded by then, fully replaced by annoyance and the ego of the man before her. "Noted. Now, if you'll excuse me, I've got important things to attend to anywhere but here."

Pushing past him, Paige was a little surprised he didn't try to physically restrain her until she heard his voice again behind her. "I'm sure you do," he said loudly enough anyone on the street would hear him. "After all, we all know the restaurant isn't the only way you're supporting yourself in this town."

Paige whirled around, using every bit of self control she had not to close the distance between them and punch the man in the face. Folks who milled about, including the boys playing baseball, watched the two of them with wide eyes. "Just what are you insinuating, Mr. Gray?"

"I'm not insinuating anything, I'm flat out saying it. There's a lot of lonely men in this town, and you're the only single woman." His eyes flicked behind her and his lip quirked up. "Can't say I blame you for not wanting to settle down with Hart - surely you can make more than a ranch foreman." He eyed her up and down, leaving no doubt in anyone's mind exactly what he meant.

Any remaining control snapped, and she took a step forward just as a hand from behind her took her arm, and another imposing figure stepped around her towards Donnie. She barely registered Riley's tall frame jogging towards Donnie before he reared back with his left hand and landed an impressive punch to the man's abdomen. "You just never learn, do you Gray?"

"I knew you were there," Donnie grunted. "I thought Pratt was fun to rile, but you're my new project." He swung and connected with Riley's cheek, but it didn't even appear to bother him with the way he tackled Donnie to the ground.

Realizing a hand still held her back, she glanced back to see Liam shaking his head. "Aren't you going to do something?"

"Guess I should, but I told Riley I'd give him twenty seconds before I stepped in. Which," he checked his watch, "time's up. All right gentlemen, break it up."

"All right gentlemen," Liam said in his authoritative sheriff voice. "Break it up."

Riley stood and dodged the cheap shot Donnie sent his way, and spat a little blood on the ground from where the man had busted his lip. He would have liked more time, but Liam had only given him the twenty seconds, and he likely wouldn't if it had not been for the both of them hearing the vile things Donnie said to Paige.

He'd been in town that day speaking to Liam and Mr. Potts about what to expect with the trial against Randolph Shipping, but a commotion outside had pulled the three of them out of the jailhouse. Paige hadn't noticed they saw the incredible catch she'd made from across the street, but they'd stayed put on the jailhouse porch until Donnie approached her.

"He started it, Sheriff," Donnie grunted. "Everybody here saw it, too."

Just then, James Pauley and Kenny Thomas shook their heads from where they stood with the rest of the baseball boys. James was the oldest and tallest, and Kenny still held a bat from earlier. "Nuh uh, Sheriff. I didn't see nothin' but Mr. Gray yellin' at Miss Paige and Riley protecting her."

Bolstered, the rest of the boys nodded and murmured their assent. Seeing a small smile grace Paige's face despite what was sure to be anger and embarrassment, Riley vowed to buy every single one of those boys a penny candy from the mercantile. The adults on the street nodded as well, most of the men staring at Donnie with narrowed eyes.

"We don't speak to women that way here," the bank president, Charlie Thorn, said from his spot on the building's porch. "If Hart hadn't high-tailed it in your direction, I guarantee someone else would have." Other men agreed, and Donnie's face grew redder and redder as the seconds ticked by.

"I see how it is," Donnie growled as he snatched his too-clean Stetson from the ground and slammed it back on his head. "This town's as crooked as a mountain switchback, and I'm not gonna stand for it any longer." Shoving a finger in Riley's face as though that would intimidate him, Donnie glared. "You watch your back, Hart, or a gal not wanting to marry you will be the least of your worries. We all got a past, and yours just caught up to you."

The threat hung in the air, and anger bubbled beneath the surface. Riley would forever hold himself responsible for Alice's death, but he wasn't the one who'd lit the match. "Do your worst, Donnie, but leave Paige alone." His voice lowered, and he knew the heat in his own expression made Donnie's look like child's play. "And if I hear you've bothered her again, Liam won't be able to break us apart."

He meant it, too, and didn't care a lick if it ended up with him in jail. It was time Donnie paid for his foolishness, and Riley would be more than happy to deliver the blows. He wasn't a violent man, but the spoiled brat pushed every button he had.

The crowd had only grown larger at the chaos, and Riley could see the flush on Paige's face deepening. She needed to be away from the prying eyes, and he was powerless to fight the urge that propelled him forward to take her hand.

"Come with me," he said with far more calm than he actually felt with Donnie still in the vicinity and curious onlookers growing by the second. Her wide eyes swung to him, but she didn't speak. "Do you trust me?"

Wordlessly, she nodded, and that was all the affirmation Riley needed to push through the fray and put the chaos behind them. If nothing else, their destination would give her a moment to breathe, and all his reasons for keeping his distance faded into the background at that thought.

Chapter Nine

Paige and Riley emerged from the wooded trail to a sight which took her breath away. They'd only walked for a few minutes, but it felt like they'd entered another world entirely. Mountains rose around the crystal lake, pine trees dotting the landscape all the way up to the shoreline. As the mountains went higher, they cleared of trees, but snowy peaks rose from them.

A fish jumped out in the middle of the lake, startling a giggle out of her, and Riley grinned as he watched her take in the sight. "What is this place?"

"This is 'Mud Lake' because one of the founders of the town thought 'Crystal Lake' would draw too many folks wanting to settle here. A generous description is he wanted to preserve the beauty, but I think he just didn't want his space crowded." He winked, gesturing towards the beauty around them. "I like to come out here sometimes when it all feels like too much. It reminds me of a few things I tend to forget."

"What things?"

Riley didn't speak for a moment, just studied the water in front of them, and she allowed him to take all the time he needed to gather his thoughts. "How familiar are you with the story of the Israelites leaving Egypt?"

That wasn't what she'd expected him to say, but Paige's curiosity piqued. She crossed the rocky shore to a large felled log, taking a seat and patting the space beside her. "It's one of my favorites."

Moving to join her on the log, Riley resumed his study of the lake. "Sometimes, when I'm here at the lake, I think about what it must've felt like for the Israelites to stand at the banks of the Red Sea. They couldn't see any way forward, and they were being pursued from behind. The fear they must've felt - it's one I'm more familiar with than I'd like to be. I know what it feels like to run and question whether you're just running away or running towards something. I've looked over my shoulder and begged God not to let someone find me, and I've done it while grieving the known and fearing the unknown."

There was still so much about his time in Boston she didn't understand, but that had to be what he spoke of. "I'm sorry for everything you've been through. I suppose I've felt a little of that, too." She hadn't thought to be scared as she boarded the train in New Orleans, but all that courage came crashing down the first day in the mercantile.

As though he didn't even notice he did so, Riley reached over and took her hand in his. A thought pricked within her to be annoyed about the mixed signals he sent, but this felt deeper than that. He needed support, and she'd just have to pray for the Lord to protect her heart.

"I know you have," he said roughly. "And I can't tell you how sorry I am for my part in that." He sniffed, and she realized his eyes misted with the memories of the road he'd walked. "Looking out at this lake, I can't help but think about how He parted the sea before them. I know myself, and I'd have been terrified to walk through it despite the clear evidence of God's power right in front of me. So many things in my life, things that turned out to be the best thing, were the things I was scared to do. Coming out here, rebuilding my relationship with my sister after the distance, the job at the Pratt ranch, even taking the position as foreman before I felt like I was ready - it all felt like the great unknown."

That part, Paige could relate to intimately. "And yet, you did it anyway."

"I did, and each time I've had to leave behind something I thought would be my future and walk towards what the Lord asks me to do. I have to trust the waves won't come crashing down on me when I'm in the middle of the sea, and if they do, He's still with me." He sniffed again, wiping a tear from his cheek in a way that broke Paige's heart a little. "I just have to put one foot in front of the other and pray God goes with me."

And He was. Just as God had been with Riley through his walk through the Red Sea, He'd be with her, too. He'd not left her as a child when she lost her parents in the tenement fire, nor in her and Mara's short but volatile time at Uncle Rufus's. He'd not left them on the streets, and He wouldn't leave her now. "I really needed that reminder. Thank you."

His hand tightened around hers, and she heard her sharp intake of breath rather than felt it. "I'm sorry I pushed you away yesterday at the ranch. It wasn't about you." His voice cracked a little, but it remained strong and deep. "I'm already afraid agreeing to testify will put Lizzie and her family at risk, but I don't have a choice. They're part of my family already, and I can only pray my actions don't get them hurt. With you, though, I can easily see you coming to mean something to me, Paige. I'll stare down the barrel of a gun, but I won't pull you into its sights."

It made sense, and the logical part of Paige could appreciate his protectiveness. Still, it didn't mean she had to like it. "I'm a grown woman, Riley. I can take care of myself."

Lifting his head, Riley smoothed a flyaway lock of hair behind her ear, his fingers lingering long enough to raise goosebumps along her skin. "I know you can, but I won't be the reason you have to." With that, he stood to his feet and held a hand out for her to take. "Come on, if we don't go back to town soon, Mara is liable to send out a search party."

Snorting at the truth of his words, at peace despite the fact nothing had been decided, Paige took in Riley's face unapologetically. "Seems the men in this town have to learn the hard way God's been taking care of us long before any of you came along, and He's done a good job of it."

With a wink, she moved back towards the trail and lifted the front of her skirts just enough to find sure footing on the uneven ground. Rather than look back to see if Riley followed, she listened for his boot-clad feet coming up the hill as well. He didn't speak, but he was there. Paige prayed he'd ponder the truth of her words.

After Riley dropped Paige off at the Olsens' house, he shoved his hands in his pockets and studied the horizon on the outskirts of town. The lake hadn't brought peace like it always did, but there was something else there with Paige he couldn't deny. The way her dark hair twinkled with red when it caught the light took his breath away, her earnestness and compassion as she listened to his story doing the same.

So lost in his thoughts he didn't even hear Liam approach from behind, he startled a little when the man appeared beside him and started speaking. "What's your plan, Hart?" He didn't sound accusatory, but Riley didn't miss the slight hitch to his words. "I respect how you've handled the situation to this point, but you don't get to lead Paige on and then push her away over and over again."

He was right, and shame pricked the back of Riley's mind even as he shook his head. "I'm not trying to, Liam. I can see myself falling for her, but I'm not putting her at risk like that." They stood between the bank and Doctor Collins's office on the main thoroughfare of town. No one save the jackrabbits was around, but his chest still tightened discussing Boston. "Randolph has a reach that's farther and wider than you could imagine, and he wouldn't hesitate to take any steps necessary to ensure the prosecution's key witness doesn't testify."

Liam didn't speak for a moment, simply staring out at the rolling grasslands and mountain backdrop. "I can respect that, but I just can't see him finding you all the way in Mud Lake. Let her stay here when you go to Boston, but be clear with her here. If you like her, ask to court her, and I'll be plenty happy. But if you don't plan on making a move, you need to back off. Stop getting in fights with Donnie-"

"I'm not going to do that, Liam."

"I don't mean let her get hurt." Liam ran a frustrated hand through his hair. "But you didn't rush over there today like a gentleman defending a lady's honor. You ran in there like a hotheaded lover staking his claim. There's a difference, and I think you know that. I don't want to see Paige get hurt, and I'd rather you didn't either."

Riley huffed, a little annoyed at the insinuation. "There's nothing Donnie can dish out I can't take."

"I didn't mean physically hurt," Liam said as he swatted Riley on the shoulder. "You're one foot in and one foot out with her, and that's a recipe for heartbreak. I don't think you'll appreciate cookin'."

He was right, and Riley knew it, but what other choice did he have? Something about Paige drew him in, but he couldn't put her in danger. "I wish I could skip past the trial and be free to move forward how I want." Images of what it might be like to court Paige for real swirled in his mind.

Picnics by the lake.

Holding her close and spinning her around the makeshift dance floor at the barn raising dance the next night.

Long walks after church on Sundays.

Reaching over to take her hand as they watched the sun dip over the mountains at the ranch.

Playing with his niece and nephew to give Lizzie and Paul a break, giving them the chance to fall for her as quickly as he knew he would. He could picture it all, but it all felt just out of reach.

Liam nudged his side, a smirk firmly in place. "That's the thing, brother. You don't get to decide how life's gonna go, none of us do. The good news for the Christian is we know Who does, and He really seems to like it when we ask for His guidance. I didn't do enough of that early on with Mara, and I nearly mucked it all up. Don't make that mistake."

Before Riley could respond, a sound by one of the barrels behind the clinic pulled their attention. Eyes narrowed, Riley followed the sound with Liam close behind. Boot prints dotted the dirt beneath their feet, but that wasn't an indicator of anything nefarious. Could it have been an animal trying to get into Doc's trash that made the sound, or had someone overheard them?

Liam knelt in the dirt and studied one of the most prominent boot prints. "These look the newest, but they could be Doc's."

Still, even as his friend tried to calm the anxiety that flooded Riley's gut, he knew better. Doc didn't wear the same type of boots the cowboys did, and that print was nearly identical to theirs. A glance down the alley didn't yield any answers, and the weight in Riley's chest only increased. Who had overheard them, and what would they do with that information?

Chapter Ten

Paige plopped down on the grass beside Kate and Mara, all three of them a little in awe of the crowd that turned out to the ranch's barn raising. "I know they have these down South, but I don't think I ever knew anyone who'd been to one."

"Not many barns in New Orleans," Kate replied. "Samuel explained it to me as best he could, but he said it was something you really needed to witness to understand. Basically, all these men will help with the framing and building of the actual barn. With there being so much help, the process goes pretty quickly, and then we'll have supper together. Mrs. Olsen was so sweet to help me with the cooking for it, plus all the bread you brought."

Stew had donated the ingredients for Paige to make enough biscuits and sandwich bread to feed a small army, and they'd all ridden out from town with Liam and Mara that morning. "It was my pleasure. You know the smell of bread lifts my spirits better than anything else."

Her conversation at the lake with Riley the day before still weighed on her mind, but she understood his fears. It didn't mean she shared them, but there was some relief in knowing she wasn't alone in her quickly growing feelings. It was odd she felt such a connection to the man already, but one didn't always get a choice in such things.

Mara threaded her arm through Paige's and rested her head on her shoulder. "Speaking of which, you haven't told me what happened with Riley at the lake yesterday."

Where to start? As the three of them watched the men begin the process of framing the barn, her story of what happened in town with Donnie and the events that followed was punctuated by the banging of hammers and good-natured ribbing between the men. She didn't share everything he told her, especially the things about Alice, but they already knew about him needing to go back to Boston to testify against an old boss. "He's worried he'll pull me into it, and I can respect that."

Her voice trailed off, and Kate reached across Mara to squeeze her hand. "These cowboys and their protective ways." She grinned, but it was soft with understanding. "When I first got here, Samuel was terrified something would happen to me, and he already blamed himself for his mother's death despite it just being an awful accident. It took some time, but he learned to trust my safety to the Lord and the fact I'm not without my own defenses." She winked, nodding her chin towards the pasture where Starlight and Samson grazed. "You'd think shooting a mountain lion or hitting a would-be attacker with a board would do it, but he had to come to it on his own time."

Mara lifted her head, and Paige realized just how much she'd missed her big sister during the time she was alone in New Orleans. "He'll come around. Do you two have any ideas who might have sent for you? Liam and I have batted around some ideas, but none of them make much sense."

"He thinks Donnie did," Paige replied. "But I can't imagine why."

Kate shook her head. "Samuel thinks so, too, but I'm not convinced." Just as she finished speaking, her eyes narrowed at a dark brown horse with a white mane trotting towards them. She apparently recognized either the horse or the rider, though the latter was still too far away for Paige to make out. "Goodness," she said with a roll of her eyes. "What is he doing here?"

Mara and Paige exchanged a curious look, but neither knew who the rider was until he got closer. Some of the hammering slowed, and Donnie came into focus as his mount came closer. Kate pushed to her feet, but Samuel had already dropped the tools he wielded in the grass and headed their way. Samuel's Stetson was pulled low on his head, but his tense jaw was clear. "Let me handle it, Kate," he said softly as he passed.

He approached Donnie alone, though Paige didn't miss how Liam, Riley, and Paul had all ceased their work and watched with tense shoulders. No doubt, if Donnie caused trouble, they'd be there in a second. Paige caught Riley's fiery gaze, his fist clenched tightly at his side. He was holding himself back, but there was no doubt he'd relish the ability to take Donnie down.

After a few frustrated words Paige couldn't hear, Donnie mounted his horse again and rode away. Samuel visibly relaxed and turned back towards the women. He reached Kate and wrapped a hand around her waist. "If he comes back and I don't see him, come get me or Liam immediately." Eyes flashing towards Mara and Paige then back to his wife, he lowered his voice. "Don't try to run him off yourselves, please."

Kate nodded, and Samuel pressed a kiss to her forehead before returning to his post. The rest of the day went by without a hitch, save a couple of minor injuries which Paige and Clarence easily tended. Doctor Collins was in town if needed, but they'd all been so minor he hadn't been necessary.

The barn was fully framed by noon, and the walls raised a few hours later. With nearly twenty men working and the comfortable sunshine, spirits remained high the whole day. As more women and children arrived nearing supper, covered dishes in tow, Paige basked in the feeling of community she'd been hoping for when she arrived in Mud Lake.

The men finished around four in the afternoon, and they rested while the women got dishes set out. Children ran around in the tall grass, playing hide and seek with express instructions to go nowhere near Dakota's corral. Thankfully, the horse appeared to grow more comfortable with the racket as the day went on, though that might've had more to do with the copious amounts of treats Kate continued to give him on the sly. Joshua probably wouldn't have minded. She worried about the ranch's latest project, and it was clear they'd started to build trust.

"Paige," Kate called from where she set out the biscuits in a towel clad basket. "Will you run in the house and get the lemonade?"

"Will do." The ranch house was large and spacious, and Paige could see her friend's touches throughout the decor. What would it be like to wake up in a place like this? It wasn't really even the house, as beautiful as it was, but the image of her and Riley sitting outside a small cabin on the property felt like a dream better than she dared dream. Was it Riley she longed for, or was it the security he would provide?

Never in her life had she ever really felt settled, even at Hope House. Of course, she was loved there, but there had always been an expiration date on her being able to live there. Working at the Latham's, despite her love of their expensive kitchen and nearly unlimited budget for food, the hate with which they spoke to each member of the staff always had her on edge.

Still, something about Riley drew her in. His amber eyes and blonde hair made her take a second glance, and she'd always felt completely safe in his presence. After her childhood, feeling protected couldn't be overstated, but she couldn't chalk it up to that alone. No, Riley had something special which made her feel like he could easily become home if he'd only allow it.

Paige moved through the farmhouse with the full pitcher of lemonade, wondering if Riley would ask her to dance that evening. Did she want him to? Yes, as much as she wished she could control those feelings, she hoped he'd ask. The idea of moving to the rhythm of a fiddle's music with his arms wrapped around her sent a jolt through her that could only be described as giddiness.

The rest of the preparations went well, and before Paige realized it, someone had pulled out a fiddle and prepared for the dance portion of the evening. Liam and Mara took the plot of grass they'd dubbed the dance floor immediately, but Samuel took a little more convincing from Kate.

Still, within minutes, he gave in and followed his wife to the dance floor. Other couples twirled and laughed as well, while children alternated between playing games and joining their parents with sweet and clumsy dances. Watching her sister and Kate with their husbands, Paige couldn't help but feel a pang of envy. She'd accepted invitations to dance from a few of the single men there, Clarence included, but the one cowboy she'd hoped would ask her spent the whole time hiding in the shadows of the brand new barn save for when he helped Samuel light a large bonfire as the sun set.

He stared unapologetically, but he never left his spot leaning against one of the corrals. Joshua stood beside him and talked, but Paige only noticed Riley respond a few times. Mostly, he watched her, alternating between tension and relaxation depending on whether she'd accepted a dance from someone. With each passing minute irritation bubbled higher and higher in her gut, and when Clarence, the older man surprisingly agile, moved them closer to Riley and Joshua during their dance, she pinned her would-be intended with a glare which could wilt flowers.

When she and Clarence finished dancing he led her back to the spot where she'd stood for much of the night. As though pulled by some unseen force, her gaze fell to Riley again. He hadn't moved, his eyes still on her despite not approaching her a single time. Clarence's chuckle cut through her annoyance, and he elbowed her gently in the ribs. "These boys don't know how to treat a lady. They're good men, but some of 'em might need a little push."

"And how might a lady do that without scaring one off?" The more she noticed Riley watching her, his tension clear each time she danced with another man, the more her frustration grew. "Especially when that's all he ever seems to do."

Clarence crossed his arms over his chest, a mischievous grin spreading over his lips. "Well, in my day, men always had to do the askin'. I don't think it's so much that way anymore. Least, it shouldn't be."

Did she dare go and ask Riley to dance and risk being embarrassed by his rejection? Paige had never been blessed with quite the confidence of her sister, but she'd always believed she could do most anything with just a few seconds of forced courage. "You know what, Clarence? I think you're right. Wish me luck."

His guffaw wasn't the least bit drowned out by the fiddle's music. "You don't need luck," he called after her. "That man's so gone over you, he'd scale a mountain if you asked."

Riley could see the determination in the set of Paige's shoulders before she even got close enough for him to get a good look at her face. Once she did, it only confirmed she was a woman on a mission. Her lip quirked up on one side, but the rest of her was all business. Mercy, but she was pretty in that pink dress. He doubted it was hers, but whoever she'd borrowed it from ought to have just given it to her outright. There was no way anyone else could look as beautiful as she did, at least not in his opinion.

Her dark blonde hair was curled a little on the ends, pulled into clips on either side to keep it out of her face. The dress was soft pink with lace along the sleeves and neckline, but it was her face that was so striking. Pink lips, slightly flushed cheeks clear in the firelight, shining blue eyes - he knew what it meant when men said the sight of a woman made it hard to breathe.

Joshua's whistle was the only thing that reminded Riley his friends stood next to him. "I think you're in trouble."

He was, but it wasn't for the reason Joshua thought. The truth was, despite his best efforts and assurances to Liam, it was only a matter of time before he did something stupid like pull Paige into his arms and kiss her like he wanted to yesterday at the lake. Would her brown locks be as soft as they looked? Would she smell as good as he imagined?

Coming to a quick stop in front of him, Paige held out a hand. It shook a little, but her voice was firm. "Care for a dance, Mr. Hart?"

He briefly registered eyes on them, but caring was beyond him at that point. He'd watched Paige spin around the dance floor with other men all night, wishing he could knock each and every one of them to the ground. He'd clenched his teeth so hard he thought they might break, especially when Caleb Parsons asked her for a second dance which she declined. He'd only relaxed when Clarence took mercy on him and asked her himself, the seasoned ranch hand as much a father figure to him as anyone.

"I...I don't know if that's a good idea, Paige." A swift kick to his behind told him Joshua disagreed with his statement, but Joshua didn't know his reasons for refusing. "It's not that I don't want to, I just-"

The disappointment which flashed on her face was quickly replaced with determination. "It's just a dance, Riley. No one's saying vows, and I've caught you staring at me at least a hundred times today. Get out of your head and just dance with me." Her hand still outstretched, she took his unbandaged one in a tight hold. "Please." The last word had been barely more than whispered, but it was the first lick of vulnerability she'd shown since she walked over.

When she looked at him like that, there was nothing in the world which could've kept him away. "All right. One dance." Clasping her hand in his, Riley allowed her to lead him out onto the dance floor as the fiddle slowed a little. He knew it's musician too well to think it had been a coincidence, as Mr. Pruitt had been a long time member of the community.

Wrapping his arm around Paige's waist, Riley allowed himself to be swept away in the moment of holding the most beautiful girl he'd ever laid eyes on. They swayed and spun, all without breaking each other's gaze. Once, when his and Lizzie's father was still alive, he'd told Riley Hart men fell in love fast and hard, but he'd never really believed it until that moment.

As much as he tried to distance himself for her safety, there was no way Paige Brown could be anything but his. She fit perfectly in his arms, but it was more than that. He could deny it all he wanted, but from the very first day he saw her in the mercantile, his fate was sealed. When she'd bandaged up his burn, he'd gotten a glimpse of her compassion. When they walked by the lake, he'd seen her kindness. And when she'd climbed into a corral with Dakota and nearly scared ten years off his life, he'd seen her courage. It had been foolhardy, but her intentions had been good.

The Pratt brothers probably watched him as he spun her around the dance floor, both of them with some mix of hope and caution, but he didn't care. They could all watch as much as they wanted, but he'd not let her go until the dance ended. Even then, he'd only do it so she could get home to rest. If it were up to him, the two of them would march over to Pastor Olsen and exchange the vows they should've said the day she arrived in town.

Fear over the Randolph trial bloomed in the back of his mind, but his sole focus was on the beautiful woman in his arms. They'd figure it out. At least, he hoped they would. This dance, under the full moon of a cool September night and the crackling glow of the bonfire, was one he'd take with him for the rest of his life.

The ranch had a beautiful view in the daylight, and he'd seen some pretty spectacular land and waterscapes in his day, but not a single one compared to the twinkle of hope in Paige's eyes as she pressed the tiniest bit closer to him. They weren't touching inappropriately, but Riley had to fight the desire to press his lips to hers in a first kiss better saved for when they had no audience.

How many songs they danced for, he had no idea, but it felt like both a moment and an eternity at the same time. Everything came into focus for Riley, but there was no way he could tell her how he felt so quickly. She'd shown interest in him, but the stirring in his heart would surely scare her away. No, he had to be careful, especially until the trial was over.

At some point, the fiddle's melody began to fade, and he heard Mr. Pruitt's call for a last dance. He was so distracted by Paige he didn't notice Donnie approach until he'd come right on them. "Enough hogging the pretty girl, Hart. I'd like to take her for a spin myself."

Riley's whole body tensed when Paige stepped out of his hold, but his anxiety was short-lived when she crossed her arms over her chest. "She'd have to agree," Paige spat. "And she doesn't. Didn't Samuel tell you to skedaddle earlier? I'm pretty sure he did. I don't waste time with men who treat women like cattle, and you've made your character quite clear."

Donnie's stance remained relaxed, but anger flashed in his eyes. "You think you're any safer with Hart? What about when he gets thrown in jail or worse back in Boston? Or didn't he tell you he's made an enemy of one of the richest men in the country?" He leaned closer to Paige, lowering his voice. "Spend much time around him, and you might just join him."

How did Donnie know about what happened in Boston, and why did he seem to think Riley was at fault? "I don't know where you got your information, Gray, but you know just enough to be dangerous and not nearly enough to be right. Step away from Paige before we have a repeat of yesterday." If only his right fist wasn't still bandaged. He'd done some damage the day before, if Donnie's swollen nose was any indication, but not nearly as much as he could do with his dominant hand.

Just then, Samuel clapped a hand on Donnie's shoulder and pulled him back. Liam stood beside him, twirling his handcuffs around a finger. "I told you to get lost, Gray. Now, you're trespassing."

"And that," Liam said as he stepped forward, "is a crime. Now, I've been itching to lock you up for years, but I'll be courteous and allow you ten seconds to get on your horse and leave. What'll it be, Gray?"

Riley couldn't help taking a step closer to Paige as he saw the way Donnie's whole body shook with anger. "You can hide behind your friends out here, Hart, but I've got friends too. The difference is some of my friends could make life mighty difficult for you, especially if they let it slip to Augustus Randolph you found your way out here. Oh, you didn't know my family's got ties to east coast money?" He shoved his hands in his pockets, shrugging his shoulders as he did so. "Don't underestimate me, or you'll regret it."

Holding his hands up in mock surrender, Donnie walked back towards where his horse had been hastily tied to a tree. Watching him ride down the road, Riley could barely contain the anger and fear that welled up from his very core. "Liam," he growled, "is he bluffing?"

"It's possible, but his family does have ties back east." Liam shifted his weight from one foot to the other as Kate and Mara approached. "I did a little digging into the Gray's when Donnie's father passed, and it turns out they owned quite a successful horse farm in Tennessee before moving out here. Apparently, Mr. Gray had lost a good deal of other people's money in a business venture gone bad, and they hightailed it west to avoid having to pay the piper. I wouldn't be surprised if he does have connections in Boston, though we can only hope those connections are with people his father slighted."

No, this couldn't happen. Augustus Randolph was ruthless, and if he knew where Riley had gone, he'd send men to make his death look like an accident. Or worse, they'd hurt Lizzie, the kids, or Paige in an effort to keep him under control. Unable to stand there one moment longer under the scrutiny of all the onlookers, Riley ran. He knew it was childish to leave rather than face his problems, but he'd take any hit to his reputation necessary to keep the people he cared about safe.

The invitation to give his fear over to the Lord pricked his heart, but there was no way he could slow the spiral Donnie's words brought in his mind long enough to even whisper a prayer. By the time he reached the pasture, his breath came in heavy pants and his legs burned from running in his heavy boots. It was a miracle he hadn't stepped in a hole and broken his ankle.

Would he have to leave Mud Lake? Was there any other choice?

Before he could follow that train of thought any further, a gentle hand settled on his back, and Paige's soft voice somehow cut through the roar of his racing thoughts. "Deep breaths, Riley. God goes before you, and you can trust Him."

Chapter Eleven

The deep, shuddering breaths Riley sucked in sitting in the pasture broke Paige's heart. He was hurting, but it was more. This man was terrified, and she could all but see the wheels turning in his head to do something drastic. "Deep breaths, Riley." Whether she did the right thing or not, Paige didn't know, but nothing in the world could have stopped her from reaching out to touch him. "God goes before you, and you can trust Him."

Was that trite? No, she didn't think it was. One of the lessons Hope House had tried to drive home for the children was God went before them, stood beside them, and remained steadfast behind. It had comforted her, particularly in the early days of coming to know Him. No matter what she did or what fire she walked through, He wouldn't leave her. Not only that, but the Lord knew every path she'd walk, and He'd catch her if she fell.

Riley turned, his expression something Paige could only describe as tortured in the bright moonlight. "I can't put you at risk, Paige. I won't, and I won't do it to Lizzie and the kids either. I...I could never forgive myself if Randolph used one of you as bait." His head shook so quickly, she feared he'd give himself a headache. "I don't have a choice but to leave."

Rather than argue and utter reassurances in that moment, Paige simply wrapped him in a hug. As soon as her arms went around his waist, she could hear his heart thumping wildly in his chest and could feel the heat radiating off him despite his shivers. At first, he tensed, but slowly surrendered to her hold. The shuddering slowed, as did his heart, and finally his arms wrapped around her. His breaths began to even out as well, and she could feel his entire being relax.

How long they stood like that, she had no idea. It could've been minutes or hours, but she couldn't bring herself to care. Finally, Riley loosened his hold, and Paige dropped her arms to her sides. He studied her through heavy lids as though the panic had taken a great deal out of him. "Thank you."

"You're not alone here, Riley. When Kate left because she thought that would be best for everyone, what did Samuel do?"

"He organized a search party, and we went after her."

Reaching up to touch his cheek, Paige smiled softly. "And don't you think for a second we wouldn't do the same for you if you try to run. You've lost so much in your life, Riley, but you've built a family here who's with you no matter what. Don't try to face Randolph by yourself."

After a long pause, Riley took another deep breath. "I feel like such a coward."

"I don't see a coward. I see a man who lost both his parents and a woman who he'd come to feel like a second mother to him. I see a man who pursued justice so doggedly he put himself in the sights of some awful men. I see a man who had the courage to start over in an entirely new place and worked his way up on a ranch despite starting the greenest of green. I see a man who'd probably rather close himself off from the world, but he lets himself love his family to a point his niece and nephew adore him. I see a man willing to testify against Randolph despite all the reasons it scares him."

Closing his hand over the one on his cheek and holding it, Riley shook his head softly. "I just wish I could face all this like a man. I never once saw my father cry in my entire life, never saw him fall apart this way."

"Just because you never saw it doesn't mean it didn't happen, but even if it didn't, there's nothing cowardly about having something to lose. Scripture tells us Jesus wept, and somewhere along the way we've decided He's not manly enough? I don't think so. Besides, you can't have courage if you don't have fear first. You stare down thousand pound bulls and ran into a fire to save a milk cow. There's nothing cowardly about you, Riley Hart."

Their hands dropped from his face but remained joined. A light breeze picked up and drifted across the pasture as an owl hooted in the distance. The moon was so big, it looked like she could reach out and touch it from the top of the mountain. Even as she studied the landscape, she could sense Riley's eyes on her. His voice was gruff and gravelly when he finally spoke. "Thank you."

"My pleasure. Now, if all this nonsense about you leaving is past, I have a request."

His thumb stroked her hand, and the slightest twinkle appeared in his eye. "Anything."

"I want you to teach me to ride a horse." Hopefully, her very real request would distract him from the last of his lingering fear. "I've loved horses since I was a girl, but I never had a reason to ride. We walked everywhere in New

Orleans, and I've mostly walked or ridden in a rig since I arrived here."

The longing she'd always felt at the idea of letting a horse cut loose across a pasture while the wind caressed her face had only grown in the time she'd been in Colorado. For the first time since she'd come after him that evening, the ghost of a grin lit the shadows on Riley's face. "I think we'll make a cowgirl out of you, yet."

"That's it, darlin'." In fact, it was a little shocking to Riley how quickly Paige had taken to riding. Liam and Mara had brought her out to the ranch three afternoons that week, and each lesson she'd grown more and more comfortable in the saddle. "You're in charge. Don't let her push you around."

Paige grinned from ear to ear as she took another lap around the small pasture atop Daisy. The twenty-year-old mare was old and gentle, retired from ranch work for the most part. She'd been a good mount when Samuel taught

Kate to ride, and she'd been Joshua's first choice for Paige as well.

As though his thoughts conjured his friend and the ranch's wrangler, Joshua stepped up beside Riley and leaned against the fence post. "She's a natural in the saddle. It took Kate a month to get comfortable in the saddle." With a nudge to Riley's side, Joshua nodded towards a plot of land over by the stream. "I keep waiting for you to ask for my help building a cabin out there for you and Paige. What's taking you so long to close the deal? She came here to marry you in the first place, and you're not that awful to look at." He snickered, taking the good-natured shove Riley sent him in stride.

"What do you know about the trial in Boston?" Samuel had let Riley lead the way in telling the other hands about what was going on with Randolph Shipping, but Joshua was bound to hear some things.

"Not much, and nothing means anything since it didn't come from you. I heard what Donnie said at the barn raising, but it didn't seem like he knew what he was talking about."

"He didn't, but he had a few details." Riley gave him a pared down version of what had brought Mr. Potts to Mud Lake from Boston and what it would mean when he had to testify. As he told the story, Paige continued to ride circles around the pasture as Starlight and Samson grazed happily in the middle. The leggy colt, Samson, had gotten big quick, and Joshua had already begun the process of convincing the animal he could trust him.

Joshua whistled. "I'm sorry you're having to do that, but my prayers are with you as you go. Do you have any idea when the trial will be?"

"Middle of November, from what Mr. Potts said. I'll do my best to stay here and out of sight as long as I can, but Randolph has a wide reach." Eager to change the subject, Riley gestured towards Dakota in his corral. "How's your new project going?"

Dakota bobbed his head and blew out a grunt, but he looked relaxed in a way he hadn't been when he first arrived. Joshua paused a moment before replying, focus now effectively off the trial and on the horse. "He's doing pretty well, but it'll be a while before he'll let me saddle him. He did let me put a pad on him and a bridle before he kicked up a fuss yesterday, so I'd say we're moving in the right direction. Speaking of Dakota, I need to get back to work, but you let me know if you need any pointers on locking Paige down." He winked and dodged a second shove from Riley, his laughter echoing as he stalked off towards Dakota.

Paige approached again, her posture in the saddle reflecting someone who'd been riding their whole life. "Can we go faster?"

"Sure, give her a quick rest, then just nudge her sides a little more." The sight of Paige on a horse did something he hadn't expected it would. Maybe it was the realization she'd fit so well at the ranch, but he knew good and well it was more. Her smile and the freedom she clearly felt riding Daisy had him thinking about a future he'd never even imagined before he met her.

Footsteps jarred him from the image of him and Paige racing across the fields at sunset, punctuating the ride with a kiss as the sun disappeared behind the mountains. Thinking Joshua had returned to rib him some more, he was surprised to hear Clarence's gravelly bass. "Smile like that? I reckon any man with all his marbles would bend over backwards to earn it his whole life through."

Paige had let Daisy graze for a minute, and now nudged her from a trot into a canter. If he'd thought her smile captivating before, the way her whole body seemed to radiate joy as they cut through the tall grass took the breath straight out of his lungs. "She's beautiful."

"You know, there was a time I worried you'd end up like me - old and alone." Removing his Stetson, Clarence ran a hand through his thin, white hair. "I've given my life to this ranch, and I don't regret it for a second. I reckon there's more to life than smelly cowboys and cooking for bunkhouses."

"Clarence, you're the reason every single one of the ranch hands leaves here with a little softer view of God and religion. Men who swore they'd never crack open a Bible have listened to your lessons on Sunday mornings, and ones who saw the Almighty as nothing more than a mean son of a gun left realizing He cared."

The seasoned cowboy grunted, uncomfortable with the praise. "I don't know about all that, but the Lord has used me despite my foolishness."

"What do you mean?" In the moment, Riley realized how little he knew about Clarence's background. It shamed him a little, to know he'd known the man for years and never asked.

"I was once a young buck in love too, and I let fear over what her family would think of me send me running. In fact, it was a warning from her father that sent me to Colorado in the first place where I met Samuel and Liam's pa. By the time I realized what I'd done, it was too late. I wrote my brother back home in Kansas City, and he told me she'd gone and gotten engaged to a more 'suitable' man. Those weren't his words, but they were the ones her family would've used." He paused, his jaw tensing at the memories. "Don't let fear hold you back from life, Son. God has been gracious enough to let an old cowboy with a third grade education share His truth with others, but I reckon I could've done that with her by my side, too."

Clarence's words washed over Riley with the realization that's exactly what he'd been doing . Letting fear control his life, it wasn't what God intended, and even the Bible said fear wasn't from Him. "And if it all blows up in my face?" It wasn't hypothetical, and the memory of the boiler exploding aboard the *Sonia* haunted his dreams at least four nights a week.

"You ask the Almighty to do His job, and you stop trying to do it for him. He ain't givin' you fear, Riley, so let Him give you courage. You don't have to see the whole road to take the next step."

He was right, and Riley couldn't deny it. "You're smarter than you look, old man."

With a chuckle, Clarence popped his Stetson back onto his head. "And don't you forget it."

Chapter Twelve

Paige wrapped the shawl Kate had lent her tighter around her shoulders as she crossed the distance between the parsonage and the church that Sunday morning. As September flowed into October, the mornings had grown more and more chilly, the slight bite to the air a little shocking to her Southern blood. Still, the dew had started to look a little like crystals on the grasslands as it reflected the light like dancing diamonds. The chill itself seemed to clear her head as she reflected on her month in Mud Lake. In fact, it had been a little over a month, and somehow the place felt more like home than she'd ever expected when she'd left New Orleans.

Crossing the churchyard to stare out at the mountains in the distance, Paige watched a leggy, adolescent fawn scamper across the field with its mother. The new pastor would be arriving that week, so they'd arranged a goodbye service for the Olsens to honor the time they'd spent here. As busy as she'd been with work and her horseback riding lessons with Riley, Paige hadn't been as diligent as she should've been in finding a place to stay once the Olsens left. She'd have to make it a priority the next week, and in the meantime Mara and Liam had all but moved her stuff to their house.

She felt Mara's presence behind her before her sister even spoke. "It's a little bit magical, isn't it?" Wrapping an arm around Paige's shoulders, the two of them studied the landscape before them. "It's hard to believe it's real."

"Not bad for two orphans from New Orleans," Paige mused. There, bolstered by the beauty of the mountains and forests in the distance, she burrowed a bit further into her big sister's side. "I don't know if I've ever really thanked you for how you took care of me growing up." When Mara opened her mouth to interrupt, Paige reached up and covered it with her hand. "Just hush, and let me thank you. Seeing Riley's fear over everything made me realize how much burden you shouldered for me over the years. I knew you provided for me, I knew you protected me, but I don't think I ever realized just how weighty all that was for you. Thank you, and I'm glad you've got someone to help bear your burdens now."

Her sister's eyes misted, and Paige removed her hand since she'd finished speaking. "May I respond now, boss?" Mara grinned, but it was a little watery. When Paige nodded, she continued. "It was the only thing I knew to do, even when I got a little smothering. But you've already thanked me - ensuring my freedom from the Lathams was all the thanks I could ever need."

"That was simply bringing justice where justice was due. You'd been falsely accused, and there was no stone I'd leave unturned to ensure you walked free." A fire had been ignited in Paige the moment she saw Mara pull an unconscious Mrs. Latham from the fire only to have the woman turn around and accuse her as soon as she woke up. She'd always been more passive than her sister, but all passivity had flown out the window at that moment.

Before Mara could respond, the church bell rang to signal the beginning of service, and the women turned to notice Liam standing on the steps holding the door. His arms crossed over his chest, and a smirk lifted his lip as he studied his wife. "Well, aren't I a lucky son of a gun? I get to walk into church with the two prettiest girls in Mud Lake."

Mara giggled in a way Paige had only ever heard her do with Liam, and her own heart swelled. Mara had given up much of her childhood to protect Paige, and the idea she got some giddiness now had her ever in her brother-in-law's debt. Tweaking Liam on the nose, Mara pressed into his quick hug. "And don't you forget it."

The service was sweet, and more than a few handkerchiefs dabbed at eyes as folks shared sweet moments of gratitude to the Olsens. Riley sat up front with Lizzie and Paul, both of his sister's children in his lap. Coralee listened somewhat intently, but Timothy babbled quietly through most of the testimonies. At one point, he stood up on Riley's leg and began blowing bubbles with his lips, amusing himself greatly as he began to bounce. Eventually, Paul had to take him to stand in the back of the room until the testimonies finished. When they did, he made his way up the aisle with Timothy in tow, his own eyes misting behind his thick red beard.

Paul cleared his throat, momentarily granted the distraction of the change in scenery for Timothy. "Thank you to everyone who brought your stories this morning. I know for every one shared, there are a hundred more that could be told. Our love and prayers go with Hal and Minnie as they venture to Texas to be with their daughter and her children. Our loss is Pine Creek, Texas's gain, and we wish them both a long and relaxing retirement. And, as I've been firmly instructed by Pastor Olsen, it's time to look to the future. Our new pastor, Benjamin Martin, will arrive this week and take up residence in the parsonage. He has been a circuit minister for eight years, and he's ready to settle down and minister to one specific flock."

Pastor Olsen stood from his place in the front pew, wiping his eyes as he went. "Pastor Martin is a good man, and a dynamic young minister of the gospel. He's an incredible testimony of the grace of God to completely shift the trajectory of a man's life, and I know he'll do well in the role. Now," he said as a mischievous look came over him. "If only we can get him to agree to send for his own mail-order bride like others in this room."

The whole congregation chuckled, but Mrs. Olsen stood and swatted her husband with a handkerchief. "Hal Olsen," she scolded with a grin. "You scoundrel." Turning her attention to the congregation, she rolled her eyes. "Hal's been trying to convince him to do that for a while now, so y'all don't mind my husband. He's getting to the age where he forgets to mind his own business."

After another round of laughter and heartfelt prayer by Paul, they finished up and readied for announcements for the week ahead. During the prayer, Timothy had wiggled from his father's grasp and ended up back in the pew with

Lizzie. "A quick announcement that we apologize is so last minute," Paul continued. "With the injury I sustained earlier this summer and a series of illnesses for our children, Lizzie and I have let planning for the Harvest Festival go longer than we normally would have. The festival is scheduled for next Saturday. As it is, don't be surprised if we enlist your help this week, and we'd like to leave it where it is to ensure the weather doesn't turn too quickly. Not to mention, we'd like to welcome Pastor Martin right."

As they adjourned from the service, Paige caught Riley's eye, and she could swear she saw about a hundred different emotions swirling within them. He held Coralee's hand, the little girl clearly besotted with her uncle as she burrowed into his side. Paige could relate, as their horseback riding lessons had only served to further convince her what a good man he was.

"Paige," Lizzie said with a kind smile from a few pews up. "The Olsens and the Pratts are coming over for lunch today, would you join us?"

Her gaze darted to Riley's, carefully looking for any hesitancy on his part. When she saw none, her shoulders relaxed. "I'd love to, Lizzie. Thank you for inviting me."

Shuffling up the aisle towards the back doors, Paige spotted Mr. Potts leaning against a tree outside before Riley did. What was he doing here? Her belly churned with questions of what he could want, but the crowd behind her kept her from stopping and gawking. As her feet reached the grass, a strong hand at her back pulled her attention. Riley's voice, low and certain, cut through her racing thoughts. "Wait for me, here? I'll go see what he wants. Then, we can walk over to Lizzie's."

"I'll be here." Rather than stand and stew, Paige turned her attention back to the landscape on the outskirts of town. As she did, the reminder to pray twice as much as she worried pricked her heart. "Lord," she whispered softly. "Give him the peace he needs to follow Your guidance. Give him courage like Daniel as he stared down the lions, the strength only You offer."

"So, you're saying someone told Randolph where I am?" Riley's whole body ran hot, beads of sweat forming on his forehead. "Who would do that?"

Mr. Potts sighed deeply, the seriousness of the situation clear on his face. "We don't know yet, but my superiors wired me in the Denver office and told me to have you on the lookout. They also offered the chance for you to back out of testifying, but I will be honest with you that losing your testimony would significantly weaken our case."

Indecision warred in Riley as he glanced over his shoulder at Paige standing next to the church house. Images of Lizzie and her family assailed him, but his answer quickly came into focus. "I'll do it. I have to - for Alice. Randolph belongs behind bars, and her children deserve some sort of settlement for all the pain his carelessness caused."

Clearly relieved, Mr. Potts relaxed a little. "I know this comes at great anxiety for you, and we'll be happy to relocate you to a safe house until the trial. Just say the word, and I'll put preparations in motion."

As odd as it might sound, a safe house was the last thing Riley wanted. In Mud Lake, at least he could make sure those he cared about were safe. Whoever tipped off Randolph could well know about the ones he loved here, and he wouldn't risk them. "No, I need to be here. Has the trial date been set?"

"Yes, it'll be November fifteenth. We'll need you in Boston by the twelfth at the latest, and you can come by yourself or bring someone." His eyes flicked behind Riley to Paige. "If, by some chance you and your bride exchange vows before then, we can ensure her safety in Boston."

Riley's eyes narrowed. "How do you know about that?"

"I find the best way to ensure justice is served is to know everything I can about everyone involved. When your name came up as our key witness, I asked around about you. But like I said, we can keep her safe if you choose to bring her, or we can put a U.S. Marshal on duty here if you leave her behind. In fact, we can go ahead and do that if it would make you feel more confident."

Mulling over the options in his head, Riley was a little overwhelmed at everything Mr. Potts told him. "If you bring in a marshal, will they be assigned to me or the town as a whole?" He had no desire to have a lawman tailing him, but one more set of eyes in town might hinder who-ever had given up his location in the first place.

Just then, the memory of the barn raising crashed over him like a rock slide. Donnie. He'd threatened Riley, but it had been weeks since they'd heard from him so Riley figured he'd forgotten all about it. Mr. Potts raised a brow at his question, but mulled it over nonetheless. "I suppose it could be whichever you choose."

"The town," Riley replied through gritted teeth at the idea it was Donnie who'd given him up. "Bring in someone to help protect the town to pay special attention to the restaurant and the mercantile. And while we're at it, what do you know about the Gray family who lives here?"

Mr. Potts scoffed. "As in Donald Gray II and his son? That's far more than I'm at liberty to say."

Chapter Thirteen

P aige swung a rag over her shoulder and wiped her wet hands on her apron. "Thank you again for letting me off a little early to help with the Harvest Festival." The level of giddiness she felt about getting to attend such festivities was a little silly, but she'd never been able to go to the fun parades and festivals in New Orleans.

Her sister had always rightfully believed two girls alone would be ripe for the picking, and she trembled at the idea they might get separated. Before that, it was more about time and lack of money, but their parents had always done their best. Pa had always worked seven days a week to put food in their bellies, so there was just no opportunity.

With a grunt, Stew shrugged his shoulders. "You're a young girl and shouldn't spend all day in a dark restaurant kitchen. Go out and live a little, and get into a little trouble while you're at it." He winked, and Paige impulsively leaned in to hug the boss who'd become more of a friend despite his many years her senior.

"You're coming to the festival, right?" Lizzie, Mara, Kate, Paige, and a few other women in town had been hard at work planning the festivities for Saturday, and it was sure to be a good time. He'd already decided to close the restaurant that day since there would be food at the festival, and she hated the idea of him just sitting alone at his house.

"Thought I might," he groused. "But I'll have to see how I'm feeling that day. Go on now, girl. Git."

Paige chuckled and offered him a mock salute. "You got it, boss."

As she pushed through the restaurant's door into the comfortably cool early afternoon, she paused for a moment to take in the sunshine. Just as she opened her eyes, the happiness she'd felt a moment before dimmed at the sight of three men she didn't recognize staring at her with calculating expressions.

Everything in her wanted to shrink back into the restaurant and tell Stew, but she'd come to Mud Lake to make her own way, hadn't she? It hadn't worked out like she thought, but if Mara could take down three would-be attackers with a loose board, she'd not play the damsel. Narrowing her eyes, Paige did her best to convey a toughness she didn't feel. Meeting the gaze of the man in front, she crossed her arms over her chest and tilted her head to the side.

The move felt powerful, but her heart thumped wildly within her chest. Still, the men stopped staring and kept moving. One glanced over his shoulder at her, and she noted a scar on his face she hadn't noticed before. It ran from his temple down his cheek, and looked for all the world like a knife wound.

Just as the shivers ran down her spine, Riley's familiar voice sounded from down the street a little. "Paige!" He jogged to catch up with her, but both his gait and tenor were calm, so he clearly didn't catch the men staring. "I'm so glad I caught you. Can I walk you over to meet Lizzie and the girls? I've got something to discuss with you."

Earlier interaction with the men forgotten, her heart slowed a little to more to a flutter, keeping time with her stomach as they settled into a comfortable pace and Riley took her hand. "Of course. But first, how is Lizzie doing with everything regarding the trial? Have you told her and Paul everything now?"

With a sigh, he nodded. "I did, as it was the best option to keep them safe. Lizzie was surprised, and probably a little hurt that I'd kept it from her, but she understood my reasons."

"I'm glad. That must feel like a weight off your chest. Now, what did you want to discuss with me?"

He removed his Stetson with his free hand, and Paige noticed he'd removed the wrap. His hand looked so much better, though the one in hers had gone a little clammy. Was he nervous? "So," he began with a slight stutter. "I don't want to overstep, but I wondered if you'd found a place to live now that the Olsens are leaving town."

The memory of their teary goodbye that morning nearly had her eyes misting again, but she swallowed it back. "I've asked around, but there aren't many folks with extra rooms. I'm going to keep trying, but in the meantime I'm staying with Liam and Mara." Liam had agreed to sleep on the sofa in the living room and let the women share the bed, but Paige had staunchly refused. "It'll work for a few weeks until I come across something."

Jamming his hat back on his head, Riley nodded. "Well, there's a widow about halfway between here and the ranch named Mrs. Jacobs. The Pratts and I have done our best to help her keep her house up since her husband died, but she could use someone to talk to as much as anything. She's got a room available, and she agreed to rent a room to you for three dollars a week. If that's too much, I'm happy to-"

"Stop right there, cowboy. You're not paying my rent." Paige abandoned the feigned sternness and grinned up at him. "But that sounds ideal. I can walk into town easily enough, and I think I know the house you're talking about." It was a cute little cabin nestled in a grove of aspens and spruces. Wildflowers dotted the front yard, and she'd always thought the place looked so cozy.

Riley's shoulders visibly relaxed, as though he'd been expecting more of a fight. "I can talk to Samuel about letting Daisy stay at Mrs. Jacobs's house for a while, if you'd like. I don't know that I like the idea of you walking back and forth everyday."

Rather than bristle at his protectiveness, Paige appreciated it in a way she didn't when she still felt like a guilt inducing responsibility for him. "That'd be nice, but I don't mind walking if I need to."

Riley squeezed her hand lightly. "You might change your mind once the snow starts falling, but we'll cross that bridge when we come to it."

She hadn't missed the use of the word "we," and for the first time, Paige wondered if life might look quite different by the end of winter. Would their clear attraction to each other peter out when Riley's emotions weren't heightened by the anticipation of testifying, or would the removal of that stress be just what they needed to take the next step?

"Thank you for asking Mrs. Jacobs," she said softly. "I'll probably be busy with Harvest Festival preparations this week, but I'd love to go by and see her Sunday afternoon if that's all right. If she's amenable, I can move in that day as well."

The idea of spending her mornings sipping tea on the cabin's front porch felt like a dream she'd never imagined possible. Even with the added time to get to work, she couldn't wait. The sunrise views over the mountains would no doubt lift her spirits on tired mornings, and the idea of seeing baby jackrabbits hopping across the fields in the spring had a smile lifting her lips.

After a minute of daydreaming, Paige pulled herself back into reality and turned her head to find Riley staring at her as they slowed their pace and reached the mercantile. A little of the tension in his shoulders back, his eyes had darkened a little. Despite being a little lankier than the Pratt brothers, Riley Hart made an imposing figure that might be intimidating if one didn't know his heart.

She met his gaze, her stomach turning over as she wondered what was running through his mind. Just then, he lifted his hand softly and ran the backs of his fingers down her cheek. "I need you to know I'd probably kiss you right now if my sister and our friends weren't staring out the mercantile window like we're a puppet show on display."

A quick glance over her shoulder revealed the mercantile's window crowded with Lizzie, Paul, both Pratt couples, Joshua, and Clarence watching them with different variations of Cheshire cat grins across their faces. If possible, Clarence's was the biggest, and he held a thumbs up as his shoulders shook with mirth. "Go on, son," he said loudly enough to hear through the window. "Don't hold back on our account."

Liam cackled at that, but Paige didn't miss the blush coloring Riley's cheeks as he groaned. "I'm so sorry about that." His voice raised a little, likely for the benefit of their audience. "Some folks just don't know how to mind their own business."

"That's all right," she giggled. In a show of bravery which shocked even Paige, she stood to her tiptoes and pressed a kiss to Riley's cheek. "I'm not sorry at all." With that, she spun on her heel and pushed through the mercantile's door to the playful cheers of their friends. "Show's over, folks. We've got a Harvest Festival to plan."

Riley stared after Paige, surprise and complete infatuation warring within him for the top spot. As the men filed out of the mercantile, Liam clapped him on the back and waggled his eyebrows. "It's a shame I didn't actually place a bet with Samuel. I'd have been two dollars richer."

"You two almost bet on whether Paige and I would end up together?" As he realized the truth of the words, a little insecurity pricked at the idea his boss would bet against it. Did he not think it was a good idea?

Samuel rolled his eyes at his brother. "Not quite. Liam was convinced you'd say your vows before Christmas, and I thought it might take a little longer to get her to fall for you after being more or less rejected." He playfully popped Liam on the back of the head. "But you weren't supposed to know about it."

"For the record, I didn't reject her. I just needed a minute to get my head on straight." The idea any man would reject Paige with her sweetness and beauty was laughable, but he also had no plans to rush her. "And we're not technically together anyway, especially with Randolph knowing where I am now." Normally, he wouldn't speak of the trial so openly, but these men were his family. They'd stand by him no matter what, and they were all well informed about the situation.

Paul placed a hand on his shoulder and squeezed. "I know you worry about your loved ones here, but you're not alone in protecting them."

"Not to mention," Liam added. "Mr. Potts and I have already spoken this morning, and there are two U.S. Marshals on their way from Denver to help keep an eye out for any suspicious characters or activity. He's taking this seriously, as are the rest of us."

For the first time since he left Boston, Riley realized just how nice it felt to be fully supported by those around him. Now that they all knew what was happening, they'd tightened the circle even further, the safety of all involved their top priority. "Thanks, everyone. I can't believe the trial's just a little over a month away."

Paul glanced back at the mercantile. "We're with you every step, brother. Now, let's talk about why you haven't asked that girl to court yet?" His eyes twinkled behind his bushy red beard, and he wrung his hands like a child on Christmas morning.

"Did we not just finish talking about the trial? I'd rather not put more of a target on her back than already exists, especially because we still don't know who gave me up." Of course, everyone assumed Donnie had been responsible, but they couldn't rule out that Mud Lake housed other moles with connections to Boston.

Clarence shook his head. "No boy, we just finished assuring you that Lizzie and Paige are both safe here, and you just got through realizing you weren't alone in all this. Not to mention, I thought we'd discussed the Almighty don't like it when we try to do His job for Him. I can assure you, son. He's better at it than you will ever be."

Memories of his conversation with Clarence about regretting letting fear drive decisions came back to him. Before he could respond, Samuel spoke up. "We're not trying to rush you, Riley. You and Paige can move as slowly as you both want, but we don't want you to think all this is on your shoulders. It's not, and as long as you'll let us meddle in your life, it won't be."

With a snort, Liam crossed his arms over his chest. "He doesn't have to 'let' us do anything. Face it, Hart. You're stuck with us. Meddling is one of my most special talents."

"You got that right," Samuel mumbled.

As the good-natured ribbing continued, Riley spotted Paige through the mercantile's window. The women still stood there talking, no doubt discussing some version of the same thing the men were. Still, as though she'd sensed his appraisal, Paige's head turned just enough to catch his eye and wink. The breath left his lungs with a whoosh, and he realized just how gone he'd already become over the woman before him. Despite his best efforts, the Lord had continued to guide them together in ways Riley never expected.

"Yep," Liam said as he followed Riley's line of sight. "I sure wish we'd actually made that bet."

Chapter Fourteen

"I give up," Mara groused as she tossed the pile of leaves and colorful ribbon on the ground. "I am just not good at crafts, and this ribbon won't stop curling up on me when I try to tie in the leaves."

The group of women sat in the back room at the mercantile working on decorations for the Harvest Festival. Lizzie painted a large welcome sign while Paige worked on bouquets of dried wildflowers. Kate carved pumpkins, and Mara wrestled with her attempt at a makeshift bunting made from leaves and autumnal fabric scraps. Somehow, she'd gotten leaf scraps in her hair and crumpled twice as many leaves as she'd managed to attach.

Paige giggled and took the needle and thread her sister held before she hurt herself or someone else with it. "Why don't we switch? You can certainly do bouquets."

"You'd think," Mara grumbled as she snatched the flowers from Paige's hand. "But apparently, I wasn't blessed with the ability to create beauty out of foliage and scrap items the way the rest of you seem to be."

Sitting back on her heels, Lizzie raised a brow at Mara. "Umm, have you seen my poor excuse for a sign?"

It was the first time Paige had looked closely, but her friend's attempts to paint leaves and pumpkins looked more like globby red and orange handprints. At some point, Lizzie had apparently smeared some brown paint with her arm, but the overall effect was readable. "It's perfect. Besides, if anyone teases you, you can just say Coralee helped."

"That is a benefit of having small children," Lizzie chuckled. "And I could probably have her do a few squiggles to keep myself from actually having to lie." Her brows went up and her mouth opened. "Oh, does anyone know what time it is? Pastor Martin is supposed to be arriving around three today. Paul's going to show him to the parsonage."

Kate glanced at her timepiece. "It's a little after two, so he should be getting here soon. When is Paul going to stop pretending he's just a shopkeeper and get the ball rolling on a run for mayor? He basically does everything a mayor would do anyway, and at least this way he'd have a little more official authority."

"I've asked the same thing," Lizzie answered with a sigh. "He loves to serve this town, but he's afraid it would take up too much of his time while the kids are still so young. He wants to be present in their lives rather than just a passing ship on his way to more responsibilities."

Paige smiled softly. How blessed Timothy and Coralee were to have such a good father. Unbidden, the knowledge Riley would be an equally good father sprung to mind. "He's got his priorities in order. There's always more time as the children get older."

Wrapping a ribbon around a passable flower bouquet, Mara nodded. "Absolutely. He's just where he needs to be." She held up the bouquet and studied it before placing it in a jar. "There, that'll have to do. And maybe next time, you girls will put me on organization and volunteer enlistment where I'll actually excel."

"She's right," Paige said with a snort. "Strong-arming people into doing things they don't want to do is Mara's greatest talent." Dodging a stem her sister threw her way, all the women broke into giggles they couldn't pull themselves out of until Paul's deep voice sounded from the door to the storeroom.

"Oh dear," he said with a grin. "Pastor Martin, I'm afraid we've caught them at a bad time. I thought for sure we'd find four grown women in here rather than school-girls." His smile only grew larger as he took in Lizzie's sign. "Dusting off those painting skills, dear?"

Shooting her husband a mock glare, Lizzie stood to her feet and closed the distance between them. "We've decided to let Coralee help with the sign when she wakes from her nap. That way, I can honestly say a three year old was partially responsible." Wiping her paint dotted hands well on her apron, Lizzie turned her attention to Pastor Martin. "Welcome, Pastor. We're delighted to welcome you to town. Pastor Olsen spoke so highly of you."

As her giggles finally died down, Paige got a good look at the clergyman. Objectively, he was incredibly handsome. His face was clean shaven, exposing a dimple on his right cheek which seemed to light up his whole face. He had dark brown hair, almost black, and appeared to know his way around hard work if his build was any indication. In another time, Paige would've been nervous at the sight of such a striking man, but somehow he didn't hold a candle to the kind rancher who'd stolen her heart.

That realization stunned her a little, but she recovered enough to join the rest of the women in introducing herself. Pastor Martin seemed kind, albeit a little overwhelmed by the gaggle of giggling women he'd walked into, but he took it all in stride. After introductions were made, the two men ventured back out into the mercantile, and Paige heard the bell above the door jingle as they left.

"My goodness," Lizzie said as she began to clean up her paint supplies. "It's a shame there's not more single women in Mud Lake. I can't say I've ever seen quite such a handsome man of the cloth."

Mara snorted, finishing up the last of her bouquets. "We'll be sure to tell Paul you think so."

"That's what happens when you've been married as long as we have," Lizzie replied. "Rather than hide the fact you think a man is handsome, you discuss it over dinner and plot whether there are any eligible young women around for said handsome man. It's really a public service, after all."

Riley had been in town more in the past month than he probably had in the last year combined. He normally tried to make it in a few times a month, plus weekly church services, and to see his niece and nephew, but Paige's presence in town had him drawn there like a moth to a flame. He woke up early everyday to finish everything Samuel needed from him on the ranch by mid afternoon, and volunteered to go into town every time Kate or Samuel voiced they might need something.

That week, as Kate had needed to come into town more often than usual for preparations for the Harvest Festival, Samuel graciously allowed him to tag along and hadn't teased him nearly as much as Liam would've had the roles been switched. By Friday of that week, Kate said they were nearly finished with everything they needed to do, and the only thing left was to cart everything from the storeroom at the mercantile to the churchyard.

He hadn't met the man yet, but Pastor Martin appeared to be enthusiastic about hosting such a goat roping of an event in his first week in town. Paul said the man was excited about the community outreach, as being a circuit pastor hadn't allowed him the opportunity to that point.

The three of them reached the church yard just as a man around Riley's age took a crate from Paige and set it on the steps. Lizzie and Paul had already begun setting up booths to their left, and he vaguely registered Liam and Mara hanging a sign to his right, but Riley's attention flew to where Paige sweetly thanked the man with thick dark hair and laughed softly.

"That's him," Kate said to both Samuel and Riley as her eyes darted back and forth between them. "That's Pastor Martin."

Samuel pulled the rig to a halt just as Riley felt the unfamiliar stirring of jealousy in his belly. Nothing about the pastor speaking with Paige was improper. He felt no need to step in to protect her, but he felt the twinge in his jaw nonetheless. A small part of him knew the reaction was ridiculous, but he couldn't seem to convince the rest of his body.

Chuckling, Samuel moved around the rig to help Kate down just as the woman in question hopped out herself. "Better get a move on, Hart. Claim her before someone else does."

Kate swatted her husband's shoulder. "She's not a homestead to be claimed by the first one who gets there. She's a woman to woo and romance."

"Fine, 'woo' her before someone else does," his boss said as he wrapped his arm around Kate. "You've got a head start, seeing as she's your bride and all." He gestured to the scene before them, as the churchyard had already begun to transform into its Harvest Festival grandeur. "Plus, dancing with a pretty girl under the moonlight seems like a good way to start."

Chapter Fifteen

There couldn't have been a more perfect day for the Harvest Festival. Somehow, despite the last minute nature of it all, they'd pulled it off. Paige and Riley approached arm in arm with Mara and Liam trailing behind. He'd insisted on picking her up at Mara's house despite her assurances they could meet there, but it seemed important to him.

Not that she minded. Come to think of it, Riley hadn't so much asked to escort her to the festival as he had simply started making plans. Mara would've bristled at such boldness from a man, but Paige found the assertiveness regarding his feelings for her endearing. In fact, since their riding lessons started, Riley had been more and more obvious regarding his interest in her. Still, they'd not discussed the Harvest Festival until after the group finished setting up the evening before.

"You ladies did an incredible job," Riley said as they stepped into the thick grass of the church yard. He wore his Sunday best, black pants with a crisp white shirt and black suspenders. The outfit was simple, but the man in it was an imposing presence in the best way. He'd also shaved his scruffy beard, something which shocked Paige when she'd opened Mara's front door that day. "You should all be proud of yourselves."

His eyes cut towards the two U.S. Marshals standing as unobtrusively as they could near the edge of the church-yard. They'd arrived yesterday, and Riley had spread word through Paul and Lizzie to the rest of the townsfolk so they wouldn't be alarmed. Mara told her it wasn't himself Riley was concerned for, but Lizzie's family and Paige. That concern, especially when he had so little for himself, had a dozen different emotions swirling within her all night long.

Eventually, she'd just had to give the whole mess to the Lord and ask Him to protect Riley and give them all peace in the situation. As she glanced up to find him studying her, she realized just how faithful God had been to do just that. "It was more fun than I ever imagined it would be, and we couldn't have done it without all your help yesterday."

Before Riley could respond, Pastor Martin approached their group with a wide grin. Paige felt the muscles in Riley's arm tense, but he relaxed quickly. For the pastor's part, his eyes darted down to the sight of their arms joined, his smile never faltering. "Afternoon, folks. I was just telling Lizzie how much I'm looking forward to today's festivities." Gesturing towards the clear blue sky, his smile only broadened. "The Lord has blessed us with a beautiful day to enjoy the fellowship, and I can't thank all of you enough for your part in putting it together."

The young pastor was kind and personable, not to mention handsome. She had no doubt any single women who came to town would fall all over themselves to get him to take notice, but Paige felt no such inclinations as she returned his sentiments. "We're pleased to be able to do it, and we hope you feel as welcome as you are."

Riley held out his free hand to shake the pastor's, his muscles slightly tensed again. "I didn't have the opportunity to shake your hand yesterday, Pastor. Riley Hart, foreman at Samuel Pratt's ranch. Welcome to Mud Lake."

"Thank you," Pastor Hart said as he took Riley's handshake. He jerked his head down in a nod as they shook, but nothing else seemed out of place. "Well, I'd better get to mingling, though Heaven knows how I'm going to remember all these names."

Liam's voice sounded from behind them. "Don't worry, Pastor. We'll help you out."

"Please," Mara said with a scoff. "Liam is a prankster, so be sure you don't ask him to jog your memory. He'll likely give you fake names just for a laugh."

Pastor Martin's shoulders shook with laughter as he looked over their shoulders to another group arriving. "I'll keep that in mind."

Folks continued to file into the churchyard, even those not part of their regular congregation. It made Paige smile to look around at all the folks who didn't regularly make it into town for church bowing their heads as Pastor Martin led them all in a prayer before the meal, not to mention enjoying time at the church in general.

Mr. Pruitt pulled out his fiddle after dinner, and they lit the candles and lamps. Riley led her to the area in front of the makeshift stage. He'd been right earlier, the festival did look amazing. Pumpkins lined the stage, as did the bouquets Mara put together. Lizzie's sign welcomed folks there, but the banner Mara had abandoned looked so pretty behind Mr. Pruitt. Children ran and played, their laughter echoing in the night air as the mountain shadows cocooned the town.

Paige took in the fun around her, tears springing to her eyes at the thought of how different this place felt than her life in New Orleans. Sure, she'd had some wonderful times there. The folks at Hope House were as gold as they came, but her life there had been one hardship after another. From their parents barely scraping by before their deaths to her and Mara's escape from Uncle Rufus and years on the streets. For a few years, they'd made their way on the streets until Paige's lung condition convinced Mara to find cleaner accommodations.

In fact, it wasn't until that moment Paige realized she'd not had any episodes of labored breathing since she'd arrived in Colorado, save for the beginnings of one at the ranch fire. The condition had gotten better with age to the point she often went weeks with no issues, but this was the longest she'd gone since the cough had first developed.

Riley's voice pulled her from her thoughts as they swayed softly on the dance floor. "Penny for the thoughts in that pretty head of yours?"

"I was just thinking how clear the air must be up here. I have a mild lung condition I've had since adolescence, but I haven't had any real episodes since I arrived."

Brow furrowed, Riley slowed their swaying even further. "Lung condition? Is that why you were coughing the day of the fire? Why haven't you told me about it before? I've pushed you hard during your riding lessons. I could've-"

"Slow down, Riley." His concern was sweet, but not necessary. "It doesn't affect my life much, obviously, as I haven't had an issue in the nearly two months since I've been here. Even at its worst, I still had a much more mild case than some of the children at Hope House. Mara doesn't even hover about it, and you know how overprotective she can be." Paige winked, hoping to ease some of the tension in Riley's shoulders.

He sighed, relaxing somewhat. "Tell me more about your life in New Orleans."

Their dancing sped up a little again, but it wasn't exactly the venue for deep talk into the hardships of her adolescence. Instead, she glazed over some of the more shocking parts. "Mara and I grew up with loving parents, but we were poorer than church mice." She grinned a little at the Southern saying, remembering her mother using it on occasion. "Pa did his best as a bricklayer, but he wasn't home much. Still, we were cared for, and Ma kept our tenement apartment as tidy as she could." She held back a shudder at the memory of the place and all the insects and rodents that made their way inside.

"How did you end up at Hope House?"

Part of that story certainly wasn't dance floor conversation, and if Riley got so worked up at the idea of her condition, he'd no doubt erupt at Uncle Rufus's misdeeds. Mara had protected her from most of what that evil man did, but it had left scars on Paige as well. "We moved around a little until Mara decided we needed something more steady. Hope House was so kind to us, and we'll forever be grateful for all the Lord did there."

Riley could see plain as day there was much more to Paige's story, but now probably wasn't the time. He'd learn, though, as he wanted to know everything about the woman in his arms. As much as he knew some of the things she and Mara had been through would make him want to put a fist through a wall, he'd listen and control himself.

As the stars shone overhead and the fiddle music slowed, he'd simply live in the moment. What would happen before going to Boston was in the hands of the Lord, but he'd carry the image of Paige's beautiful face in his mind the whole way. Tightening his hold on her the slightest bit while still stopping short of indecent, they moved around the dance floor as though no other couples existed.

He'd never been much of a dancer, but holding Paige's soft hand in his as he twirled her around had him wishing the night could go on forever. When she stumbled a bit into his chest, her cheeks pinked in a way he knew would be even more captivating in the daytime. His heart raced, but he'd never felt so at peace. It was an odd contrast, but one he hoped wouldn't end anytime soon.

He spun her once again, her smile growing wider as he gestured for her to go around a second time. Her lips beckoned him to close the distance between them, but he held himself back for the moment. It would come, but not in the middle of a crowded dance floor. "You are the most beautiful woman I've ever seen." His voice was husky, but it didn't tremble with the emotion swirling within him.

Bringing a hand to her cheek, he did his best to catalog every detail of her. Her light brown hair curled softly around her shoulders, framing her face that belonged on a classic painting. Her skin, fair and perfect, felt like a little bit of Heaven on earth. Just as he'd lost himself in her eyes, she stood on her tiptoes and pressed her lips to his.

He froze for a second. This hadn't been the way he'd planned for their first kiss to go, but he wasn't about to ruin it. The hand on her cheek wrapped around the back of her neck to bury itself in her hair. It felt just as smooth as it looked, and it took every bit of self control within him to pull back before he took the kiss to inappropriate places.

Paige's eyes sparkled in the moonlight, and she giggled lightly. "I didn't really plan to do that."

"You won't hear me complaining," he said with a chuckle.

They danced for a while longer until both of them decided to take a rest. The church steps were empty, and it was close enough to the festivities he wouldn't risk Paige's reputation. Things were a little more lax in the West, but he'd never risk her that way. Thankfully, the steps were far enough away they could still talk without being overheard.

Riley wrapped his arm around Paige's shoulder and sighed at how right it felt as she settled herself into his side. "Tonight has been perfect," she said softly. "Thank you."

"I hope to make many experiences perfect for you," Riley said honestly.

Shifting her head to face him, Paige's eyes held compassion and understanding. "How are you feeling about the trial?"

A lifetime of trying to hide his fears to avoid being a burden to others had him wavering, but this was Paige. She deserved the truth, and there was no way they could build a real relationship if he refused to be honest. "I'm afraid."

"What are you afraid of?" Paige's tone held no accusation, only a desire to understand.

"I'm afraid of what might happen to you and Lizzie's family while I'm gone. I'm afraid my testimony won't bring justice for Alice. I guess...I guess I'm also afraid of looking like a fool on the stand. It's been years since the explosion, and I've always wondered if I could've done more to report the safety concerns." Would they somehow prove it was his fault? As ridiculous as it might sound, the possibility continued to rear its ugly head.

Paige covered his free hand with hers, squeezing it tight. "Has Liam told you anything about our childhoods?" When he shook his head, she continued. "After our parents died, we went to live with our Uncle Rufus for a time. He was cruel, but Mara took the brunt of his drunken anger."

The only thing keeping Riley's temper in check at the idea was the Almighty. "What did he do?" His words came out as a growl, but Paige didn't seem to notice.

"He'd come home drunk and want to fight. We were there, so he'd nitpick about things that weren't even our fault. Not to mention, despite the hovel he lived in before we arrived, he'd rant and rave about how we were responsible for his financial ruin. We did our best to stay out of his way, but he still lost it a few times a week. Mara could always tell when he was about to start swinging, and she'd provoke him with that sharp tongue of hers. I used to wonder why she did it, but now I know it was to keep the attention off me. Ultimately, it wasn't until he locked Mara in a closet and forced her to listen to him hurt me that we left." A tear rolled down her cheek, and Riley shook with rage at the thought. "All those beatings she took, all that pain, was it my fault?"

His jaw fell open, painful at how hard he'd been clenching it. "What? Of course not."

"Exactly. I knew what was happening, but I wasn't the one responsible." She pulled out of his hold and took his face in her hands. "What happened to Alice was a tragedy, Riley, but you weren't the one responsible. The only people to blame are the ones who ignored your reports and cut corners to save money. We can't control the actions of other people any more than we can lasso the moon and pull it closer. All we can do is live a life that honors God and leave the justice to Him. We can fight for the truth to come out, and that fight takes courage, but it's not all on our shoulders."

Mr. Pruitt called out for the last song, and Paige stood to her feet. Before Riley could respond to her words, she pulled him up as well. Assuming the same position they'd danced in earlier, Paige placed a hand on his shoulder. "Courage doesn't mean you're not scared, Riley. It means you're scared and do it anyway. There was a time in my life I wished I was more fearless like my sister. But you know what I learned? I learned not a single one of us is fearless. What scares Mara doesn't scare me, but we all have to push through whatever it is the enemy wants to convince us is real."

As they swayed in the moonlight, the shadows darkened her face to a point he couldn't read her expression anymore. "And if I've let fear control me for a long time?"

In the same manner he did earlier, Paige ran a hand down his cheek. "You remember the power of the God we serve. You remember how far He's brought you. You remember the Red Sea road He gave the Israelites and trust Him for your own."

Chapter Sixteen

"That's it now," Riley shouted to Joshua. "Release him and run while the mama's relaxed." He watched from horseback as Joshua freed one of their yearling bulls from the thicket he'd gotten himself tangled in. The animal would be sold off soon to a neighboring farm so he didn't cause any issues fighting for dominance, but for the moment, he was still at the Pratt ranch getting into trouble. An uncharacteristic storm for this time of year appeared to be rolling in over the mountains to the west, and they wanted to get him free before it hit.

Joshua half ran half stumbled backwards once the bull was freed, hopping back up onto his horse with the skill of one who'd been doing it all his life. Joshua might be their wrangler, but he didn't stay at the barn all day even when he had horses he worked with. He split his time between them and the cows, and he'd more than earned his stripes as a bonafide cowboy. Riley hadn't grown up as one either and didn't know if he'd ever have quite the cow sense Samuel had, but ranching fit him better than working the shipyard ever had.

The thought brought the trial back to top of mind. "Lord," he prayed softly as he and Joshua headed back to the bulk of the herd. "I'm trusting You'll walk with me, and I'm trusting you love my family even more than I do." Paige was included, and the Lord knew it. In fact, in the weeks since they'd talked at the Harvest Festival, he was more sure than he'd ever been that he'd be marrying Paige by Christmas if she'd have him.

Samuel had already agreed to sell him a small plot of land on the Pratt ranch. In fact, it had been one of the few times Riley had seen his generally stoic boss giddy. As they'd talked over the plans for his cabin, Samuel and Kate had made suggestions he hoped Paige would like. He'd ask her before he started building, of course, but he needed to get a ring first.

The Lord knew all that, and Riley grinned as he continued to pray. Putting the outcome of it all in the Lord's hands was the only way that made sense, and it pulled the bricks off his shoulders that had been there since Mr. Potts came into town.

Thunder rumbled in the distance, and a rider raced from the direction of town with a wagon riding at a determined pace behind. Narrowing his eyes, Riley could see the rider was Paul, and the women in the wagon were Lizzie, Paige, Mara, and Paul's mother, Betty. Coralee had burrowed into her grandmother's side, but Timothy was doing his best to break from Paige's hold. He, at least, appeared to be having the time of his life.

Whatever was happening, it was big, and Riley followed the rest of the ranch hands at a gallop to the ranch house. Even Winchester seemed to know something was wrong, as he ran at a pace rare for him. When they reached the barn, Riley quickly tied the animal in the shade of a large oak and closed the distance between him and Paul quickly. The wagon still made their way up the long drive, but they'd be there in a few minutes.

Kate stood on the front porch, wringing a towel in her hands while Samuel swung down off his mount. "What's wrong, Paul?"

"Liam sent me to bring as many men as you can. He just received word for help from the Sawyer's Pass sheriff that the train derailed halfway between there and Mud Lake. Any men you can spare, we'd appreciate it. I brought the women since all of us will be gone with Liam, and I'd rather them be safe here than in town."

With a nod, Samuel climbed the porch steps to Kate. "I'm going to leave Riley and Joshua here to watch after you ladies, but you know what to do if anyone comes out to give you trouble." Kate assured him she did, and Riley thought back to all the days he'd heard Samuel giving his wife shooting lessons. She was a pretty good shot, particularly for never having touched a firearm until she married Samuel. "Riley, do you think you two can get the herd ready for a storm on your own?"

"Yes, sir."

Mara hopped out of the wagon, taking Timothy from Paige and extending a hand for Coralee. "We'll be fine, Samuel. Y'all just go help my husband before he does something foolish like ride off all by himself."

All the men but Riley and Joshua took off towards town, but unfortunately the two of them wouldn't be able to stick close to the house like they'd prefer. Helping Paige down from the wagon first, then Lizzie, Riley addressed the two most important women in his life. "You ladies fire off a shot if anything's amiss, alright?" For some reason, his gut churned with something deeper than normal fear. He didn't have the time to try and discern what it was, but it didn't make him any more comfortable leaving them alone.

Mud Lake wasn't a lawless town, but there were more than a few men who'd try and take advantage of women alone while all their men rode out with Liam. Paige took his hand and squeezed, eyeing the storm that rolled in around them as the wind started to whip the hair that had fallen from her bun. Her face was flushed from riding so quickly from town in the chilly weather which grew colder by the minute, her eyes shining as they watered. "We'll be fine. You go tend to the herd."

Just as Samuel had done to Kate, Riley leaned down to kiss Kate's forehead. As he did so, thunder rumbled in the distance, and the wind picked up. With a quick nod to Lizzie, he jogged back to where Winchester pawed the ground in clear understanding something was wrong.

The wind threatened to pull Riley's Stetson from his head as it continued to blow, and he tightened the strings around his chin. Looking back at Paige would no doubt set his gut twisting again, but he couldn't help himself. She'd pulled her shawl close around her, a soft smile didn't quite reach her eyes, which had Riley wishing he could forego all his responsibilities and pull her into his arms.

But he couldn't, and they weren't without protection there at the big house. Not only had Samuel taught Kate to shoot, but Mara had come to Mud Lake already knowing how. They'd fire a shot if they ran into trouble, and he and Joshua could be there in minutes. Still, as Riley and Joshua rode back out to tend the herd and drive them under a cluster of trees in case the storm brought hail with it, he couldn't help but feel like it wouldn't be that simple.

"Paige," Mara chided softly. "If you don't stop pacing, you'll wear a hole in the ground. They're fine. Storms happen, and Riley's been handling the herd during them for years."

Lizzie stood and crossed the room to take her hand. "Mara's right. Riley's got a natural cow sense that would beat all you've ever seen. He doesn't believe enough in his own abilities sometimes, but whatever comes up out there, he can handle it."

She couldn't explain it, but Paige couldn't shake the feeling something wasn't right. Riley was set to leave for Boston in three days, so that could be what had her jumpy, but she didn't think so. "I'm going to go out and check on them."

"Paige," Kate said firmly. "That's not a good idea. Riley can't focus on what he needs to do if he's worried for your safety." Just then, the thunder clapped and shook the window panes. The sound of hail on the roof had Paige's heart sinking to the floor, and a crack of lightning lit the dark sky.

Kate was right, and Paige knew she should heed the warning. Still, it was as if another force had her swinging open the door. "I'll just climb up to the barn loft and see if I can spot them," she called over the gale. "That'll be enough to calm my nerves."

The sounds of Coralee and Timothy playing in the parlor reminded her of the safety behind her, but nothing could have kept her from stepping out into the storm. Unfortunately, she didn't even make it to the barn when the sight of Riley and Joshua's horses put an image to the dread she felt. Neither had riders, and both looked highly agitated for seasoned ranch horses.

They stood outside the barn, both pawing the ground and snorting as they spotted her. Winchester whipped his head up and down, and Paige ran over to the pair. "Oh, Lord," she begged as the rain pelted her head and shoulders. "Please let them be alright." Not willing to waste one more minute, Paige thundered back towards the house. "Their horses came back without them! I'm going to look for them."

With a determination that hadn't been there a moment before, Mara shot to her feet. "I'm going too."

"Me too," Kate said quickly. "Let me get some of Samuel's clothes for us to wear so we're not slowed down by our dresses." She rushed off towards their bedroom, just as Lizzie handed Coralee to her mother-in-law.

"I'm coming." She leaned down to press quick kisses to her children, exchanging a silent conversation with Paul's mother before wiping a tear from her cheek.

Lizzie was Riley's sister, but she was also a mother. "Are you sure you want to come?"

"He's my little brother," she replied with a voice of steel. "I'm coming."

Five minutes later, the four of them stepped out into the storm swallowed by Samuel's clothes. Some of them fit better than others as they'd belonged to the Pratt boys as adolescents, but they were all much bigger than the women needed. Kate wrenched open the barn door as Winchester and Joshua's horse followed her in. "I'll feed these boys while y'all get two more tacked up. Lizzie, how well do you ride?"

Riley's sister bit her lip and shook her head. "Not well, I'm afraid, but I'll manage."

"That's fine," Kate replied. "You can take Daisy. Mara, you take Winchester." She raised a brow at Paige then, her eyes darting to the stall where Dakota stood. "Joshua's made great progress with him, and unfortunately most of our horses are out with the men. Starlight still isn't ready to ride, so one of us will need to ride Dakota. He's still temperamental, but a strong rider can handle him. I've seen you out here with Riley, and somehow you surpassed my skills in your first few lessons."

Grabbing a bridle off a nail on the wall, Paige jogged to Dakota's stall. "I'll take him." Lowering her voice to a reassuring whisper, Paige stepped onto the hay. "All right, boy. I need you to trust me because I need to be able to trust you. If you help me find Riley, I'll give you all the carrots you want."

Without waiting for a response, Paige placed the bit in Dakota's mouth and breathed a sigh of relief when she didn't get bitten. The thunder pounded overhead again, but thankfully the rain hadn't soaked the ground yet. Tracks would be the only possibility of their locating Riley and Joshua quickly, and a deluge would wash them away.

They finished tacking up and mounted in minutes, letting Kate lead the way to the pasture where the men had been working. "Lord," Paige prayed again. "Help me do what I've been telling Riley to do for months. Help me trust You with his safety. Lead us to them, and give us the wisdom to know what to do."

Kate holstered two pistols at her hip and strapped a rifle to her saddle. Mara did the same, while Lizzie tucked a hammer into her saddle bag. Frustration at not having learned to shoot over the years washed over Paige, but she swallowed it down and grabbed a tool she couldn't even identify off the wall. It had a wooden handle and a long metal rod with a hook on the end. It was heavy enough to pack a punch, and that was all she really needed. At the last minute, she grabbed a sheathed knife from the barn wall as well.

They'd do their best, and they'd trust God to lead them. It was the only thing they could do, but it was also their best chance at bringing the men home alive.

Chapter Seventeen

R iley woke from a stupor to a nudge to his ribs. "Riley," Joshua's voice hissed. "Riley, wake up."

Why was he asleep? Why did his head hurt something fierce? Did Winchester get spooked and throw him? Feeling the scratch of ropes on his hands, realization washed over him. He'd had his back to the wood line counting to be sure all the herd were accounted for when something large and blunt had struck him in the back of the head. He'd fought to stay awake, but the last thing he remembered was slumping forward in Winchester's saddle and beginning his descent to the ground.

Wrenching his eyes open, he did his best to blink out the sawdust feeling. They were in some sort of wooded camp about halfway up the mountain if his guess was correct.

Four men he didn't recognize sat drinking coffee around a fire, though the fire was a pitiful excuse in the spitting rain. They'd gotten it going, but it smoked more than anything.

Good. If Samuel and the men came to look for him, they'd see the smoke before anything. That mistake alone told him their kidnappers were likely hired men from Boston, and their accents confirmed it.

"Pass me the coffee, Wilks. I'll show you how to really make trail coffee."

The other man snorted. "How would you know? This is the first time you left the east coast in years."

Yep, Boston for sure. Which meant they were sent by Randolph to take him out before the trial. The question was why didn't they just kill him. Cutting his eyes to Joshua, he spoke as low as he could to try and avoid being heard. "Are you hurt?"

Joshua shook his head. "I came willingly when they knocked you over the head. Wasn't leaving you alone." He shrugged, and gratitude and frustration warred within Riley.

"You shouldn't have done that. You could get yourself killed."

Rolling his eyes, Joshua grinned a little. "At least we'll go down together, right? Fact is, all the men are on their way to help the derailed train. By the time I could get help, you'd be long gone. My only option was to come with you. It's what you'd have done for me."

He was right, and the reminder of the men heading to Sawyer's Pass had any hope of rescue fading. No, he'd have to play this smart since brute force would only get them both killed. He was a pretty good fighter, but they'd disarmed them both. There was no way two unarmed men could take on four heavily armed ones.

Paige's face flashed through his mind, and he wondered if he'd ever get to see it again. Lightning flashed and thunder clapped once again, the rain and hail coming down harder on their heads. At least they'd let them keep their hats.

The man who'd complained about the coffee stood to his feet, followed by one of the other men. The second had a scar running from his temple to his cheek, knife wound, that much was clear.

The first man knelt in front of him and Joshua, clearly more than a few years their senior. His mustache was gray, and the lines around his eyes told Riley he'd spent more than a few hours in the sun. "Morning Sunshine," he said. His voice sounded like gravel, a disturbing giddiness to it. "Now, let's have a chat."

"Randolph send you?" Honestly, the fear didn't rise up to choke Riley the way he might've thought. It was him they'd taken rather than Paige or Lizzie, and that didn't hold near the desperation the alternative would. He could keep a clear enough head under such circumstances.

A grin spread across his face. "Smart boy. Yep, he's got a message for you."

"A message? That's it?"

That was apparently a step too far, as the scarred man's hand fisted and planted itself firmly into the side of Riley's face. "You'll be quiet if you know what's good for you."

"Easy, Stripes," the leader said. "He ain't hurting my feelings."

Thunder pounded again, and the wind kicked up even further. Their captors didn't wear the thick leather coats Riley and Joshua wore. That was another clue they were from Boston, and they had clearly underestimated the Colorado cold as the other two men were frantically trying to keep the fire going despite the weather . "Why don't you just tell me Randolph's message?"

"A man who cuts to the chase - I like it. Fine. Here are your options. You can either come back to Boston with us and testify you made the whole report up, or you meet a mysterious and tragic end tonight. Unfortunately, so does your friend."

To his credit, Joshua didn't look nearly as afraid as he ought. Still, Riley wouldn't put it past the men to dispose of Joshua for the sake of simplicity. "Let him go, and I'll go with you." There, he didn't say he wouldn't flip on the stand. If he ended up with a bullet in his chest, then so be it. He'd have died with his integrity intact. The image of Paige grieving his death hovered at the corner of his vision, but he refused to allow it the room to set in.

Before the man could answer, a gunshot behind them sounded, and the thundering sound of horse hooves told him the cavalry had arrived. At least, he hoped it was the cavalry. Judging by the shock on both men's faces, they were in the dark too.

The scarred man received a bullet to his shoulder just as he went for his gun, his good hand going straight to the wound as he howled in pain. His boss went for his gun just as a rider on a familiar horse barrelled into the clearing and whacked him on the head with what looked like a large bale hook. Was that horse Dakota?

Realization hit him between the eyes just as he felt the ropes behind his back loosening before freeing him. His head whipped around to see Lizzie in full men's clothing with a knife in her hand sawing at Joshua's ropes. "Lizzie? What are you doing here?"

"We can talk about that later, little brother. For now, you might want to go help the others." Riley followed her line of sight to the image of Paige atop Dakota swinging the bale hook right at the gut of one of the men who still stood by the fire. Joshua had already started towards the women, and Kate tossed him a pistol.

Sprinting their direction, Riley's gut sank at the sight of the man Paige had just hit in the gut pulling his gun. On sheer instinct, he barreled forward and tackled the man to the ground, bracing himself for the impact as he heard the gun fire. When the sharp pain of a bullet wound didn't come, Riley registered the man below him had stopped struggling.

Blood poured from the man's head, and Riley looked up to find Mara's shooting hand still raised. It shook a little, but she lowered it while sliding her mask of toughness back in place. "Is he dead?"

"He is," Riley answered softly. He knew what it would do to Mara to know she'd killed a man, even one who'd been about to shoot her sister. Unfortunately, they didn't have time to dwell on it because the scarred man had pulled his own gun with his other hand and pointed it in Riley's direction. Before he could fire, Lizzie swung a hammer from behind him, and he slumped to the ground. At least he didn't appear to be dead, something Riley would never wish on his sister's conscience.

The older man who'd appeared to be in charge lay still on the muddy earth, but he was breathing too. The only kidnapper left had been the second one who'd stayed by the fire, the one who'd proclaimed he could make better coffee than the others. His eyes went wide, and he held up his hands in surrender. "Don't kill me. I'll cooperate."

Kate swung down off Winchester with a gun trained on the man while Joshua pulled a pistol from the man's holster. "Lay on your belly, and put your hands behind your back." Rather than make any of the women tie him up, Riley rushed forward to do the honors. He didn't have cuffs, but there was plenty of rope left from where they'd tied him and Joshua.

Between the rest of them, they gave the same treatment to the other two living henchmen and had just finished securing them when the sound of more horse hooves pounded from the direction of the Pratt ranch. Samuel and Liam led the way, both faces stony with worry.

As soon as they spotted their wives on their feet, Riley could see their shoulders relax the slightest bit. They dismounted, and both Pratt brothers and Paul rushed to their wives. Joshua elbowed Riley gently with a smirk. "You'd think it was the women who got kidnapped."

Giving back a friendly shove, Riley left Joshua and moved towards Paige. Her face had gone pale, and her hands shook just like Mara's, but she was breathing and in one piece. "I thought we were too late," she breathed. "I thought they'd already killed you."

Unable to hold back another second, Riley pulled Paige into his arms and stroked her back softly. "I'm right here, darling. I'm safe, and it's because of you ladies."

Liam was in a similar position with Mara, but he took on the mask of a lawman then. "What happened?"

Both U.S. Marshals assigned to protect Riley's loved ones had also ridden in with the posse, and they dismounted as well. "We'd like to know that as well."

Paige sat next to Mara on a log by the dwindling fire as Joshua and Riley filled the lawmen in on what had happened prior to the horses coming back without them. Once they finished their part of the story, Lizzie picked up the rest.

"The worst of the rain held off long enough for us to find their tracks, and we followed them for a ways until the bottom fell out. At first, we feared we'd completely lose the trail, but Kate spotted the smoke from the campfire. We took the chance it was them, and we followed the smoke up the mountain. We actually found them a few minutes before we rode in, but we paused to get our bearings around that outcropping over there. We debated keeping them in our sights and sending someone back down the mountain to get help. Then one of them punched Riley, and Paige refused to wait any longer."

Hands settled on Paige's shoulders, and Riley's scent and comforting presence filled the air around her. He gently massaged the knots of tension from her shoulders before speaking. "They were definitely sent by Randolph. My options were to die today or go with them to Boston and recant everything I told the police then. They wanted it to look like an accident."

"And that," Joshua said, "is when the ladies rode in and saved our behinds."

Kate shook her head from her spot firmly tucked into Samuel's side. "So what happened with the train derailment? Was that just a diversion?"

"Yep," Samuel said through gritted teeth. "We got to Sawyer's Pass, and the sheriff there had no idea what we were talking about. I have a suspicion who sent the phony wire, but it'll take us some time to prove."

Just then, the unharmed kidnapper twisted his head around in the dirt to face them. "No, it won't. The guy who tipped off Randolph and met us at the train station is the same one who sent the wire. Donnie Something-Or-Other."

"Of course," Liam growled. "As soon as we get everyone back safely, I'll head over to his house to make the arrest. Marshals, will you help me transport these hired men?"

They confirmed they would, and all the men chipped in to secure the criminals to different horses. Just as Paige stood to stretch out her stiff muscles, she spotted Dakota bobbing his head up and down. "Hey boy," she cooed as she approached slowly. "You were amazing."

A hand at her back had her turning her attention to Riley who also ran a hand down Dakota's neck. "You sure were." He twisted Paige a little in his arms, his eyes full of emotion. "And so were you." Lowering his lips to hers, Riley told Paige everything he was feeling without speaking a word. When he broke the kiss, he ran a thumb gently across her lips. "Thank you for being stronger and more capable than I've ever given you credit for. I'm sorry for that, and I'm sorry for putting my failure to trust the Lord on your shoulders."

His sincerity stirred her heart, and Paige fought the urge to kiss him again. "We all have our hang ups, and there's grace for them all."

"Maybe, but I think I figured out what my Red Sea road is, the thing that shows me the goodness and faithfulness of God despite all my fear." He ran the backs of his fingers down her cheek, leaving a trail of goosebumps in his wake. "It's you, Paige Brown. You're my Red Sea road. The Lord used you to lead me out of the prison of fear. I'm not saying I won't fall back into it, but one look at you will remind me of everything I tend to forget."

Pushing to her tiptoes, Paige closed the distance between his lips and hers once more. It was short, a chaste and gentle kiss, but it felt much deeper. It was a promise of things to come, and a reminder of all God had done.

Chapter Eighteen

Riley followed Mr. Potts out of the imposing Boston courthouse into a blinding sun reflecting off the dusting of snow they'd gotten overnight. In the short time he'd known the U.S. Attorney, Riley hadn't ever seen him smile. At least, he hadn't until now. "You did it, son," Mr. Potts said as held out a hand there on the busy street. "It's because of you that Augustus Randolph won't get away with the death of Alice and a number of employees lost due to his carelessness."

"I'd hardly say I was solely responsible," Riley replied. Anxiety bubbled in his gut at the idea Randolph would think so, even from behind bars, but he did his best to take it captive and give it to the Lord. Never in his life had he really been able to put that verse into action, but lately the Lord had been giving him the strength he'd begun asking for. Remembering all the things He'd brought him through helped tremendously, but Riley would be glad to get back home to Mud Lake.

"Fair," Mr. Potts said as he stuffed one last paper into his briefcase. "But I don't know it would've gone the same way if it hadn't been for you. In fact, there are some folks I thought you might want to see before your train departs."

Who could he mean? "Mr. Potts, if it's reporters, I've really got to-"

The man's grin grew impossibly wider. "Nope. In fact, turn around."

Curious, Riley did as he asked and took in the faces of two of Alice's three adult children. Titus stood with a child not much older than Coralee on his hip, his dark hair and thick mustache so similar to the photo Alice had kept in their apartment of her late husband. A pretty brunette woman whose stomach was swollen with child stood at his side, her hand in his.

Katherine, the youngest, rushed forward from behind her brother, and a red haired man watching them with equal parts patience and protectiveness hung back. This must be her new husband. The middle son, Roan, wasn't there, but the last Riley knew, he'd moved out West as well.

"Riley," Katherine squealed, as she barrelled into his arms. "You were amazing."

Her words registered a moment later, and Riley's eyes widened. "You were there?" His attention turned to Titus then. "You too?"

"Wouldn't have been anywhere else," Titus replied. "I sat in the back through every day of the trial, but we brought the whole family for the verdict. Just like Katherine said, you were amazing. Thank you for bringing justice for my mother. She loved you like a son, and you did her proud."

Tears pricked in Riley's eyes as Katherine moved to stand beside her husband once more. "It was the least I could do."

Titus's friendly smile fell from his face, and he placed the child on his feet before stepping towards Riley. "Mr. Potts told us you have some ridiculous notion that any part of this was your fault. It wasn't, and not a single one of us blame you." Titus was only six months younger than Riley, and he'd taken on the role of mother and father when Alice died. Riley had done the best he could, sending money back, but it had been Titus who kept his family together.

"Thank you for saying that. It means more than you know."

Just then, the little boy pulled on his father's coat, doing a little dance as he did. "Papa, I'm hungry."

"Riley McKinley," his mother said as she pulled him back. "What have we told you about interrupting adults when they're talking?"

Riley. "You...his name is Riley?"

Titus grinned. "Sure is. I figured naming him after the bravest man I've ever known would work out well for him. He wears it well, I think." With a wink, Titus pulled Riley into a hug. "You risked everything back then to keep folks safe, and you did it again during this trial. I'd be proud for my son to grow up to be just like you."

"Paige, you're going to wear a hole in the floor," Mara scolded jokingly as they all stood on the train platform awaiting Riley's return. His train was due any minute, but it was always possible it had been delayed. Clarence and Joshua had also come into town to welcome Riley home, though the both of them looked nearly as nervous as she did for some reason.

Before Paige could reply, the train whistled in the distance, and Paige's heart pounded in giddy anticipation. It pulled to a stop just as the doors swung open, and Riley was the first one off. He bounded down the steps, his small bag in tow, and closed the distance between them in two steps. Jamming his Stetson to its rightful perch and dropping his bag, he pulled her into his arms with none of the hesitance he'd done before. "You, Miss Brown, are a sight for sore eyes."

"As are you, Mr. Hart."

He'd barely pressed his lips to hers when Liam interrupted with mock offense. "Hey, we're here too, Hart. And we have a surprise for the both of you."

Samuel elbowed his brother in the side, rolling his eyes. "Let him kiss his girl. It'll wait."

But it was too late, as Paige had always loved surprises. "Wait, a surprise for both of us?"

"Yep," Samuel replied. He pulled Kate close to his side, and one of his rare big smiles spread over his face. "One of the things keeping you back from asking her to marry you was not having a cabin, right?"

Riley nodded, his brows raised.

"We figured we'd remedy that for you. I've deeded you the land we talked about a month or so back, and all it needs is your signature. Between us, Clarence and Joshua, we've got the place pretty close to livable."

Paige's mouth dropped open as she took in her sister and Kate. "That's why you two kept asking me what things I liked about the farmhouse and what things I'd want in my own." She'd thought they were bringing up house plans too much, but she'd been so preoccupied thinking about Riley in Boston it hadn't occurred to her they might be building one. Staying with Mrs. Jacobs had been surprisingly perfect, as the ride to and from town everyday had given her time to pray and ask for peace and wisdom regarding her next steps.

Whatever those next steps were, she knew they involved Riley. Speaking of, the man in question still held her close, but his whole body seemed to have frozen. "You four built us a house? I'd planned to do that when we got back. What do I owe you for materials?"

"Absolutely nothing," Samuel snorted. "In fact, it's even gonna have a fancy new cookstove once it arrives from Denver. That one's courtesy of these two," he said as he crooked a thumb at Clarence and Joshua.

"Ahh, it ain't nothin'," Clarence said. "Besides, we figured we owed you some kind of apology anyway."

Liam bit his lip to keep from laughing as Clarence and Joshua both studied the ground. "Ask him what he's got to apologize for, Riley."

Realization washed over Riley's face as his eyes widened. "You two sent off for Paige?"

If it weren't for Riley holding her up, Paige might've dropped right there on the platform. "What? You two? Why in the world would you do that?"

"It wasn't to be mean," Joshua said quickly. "We just both knew how much Riley wanted a family of his own but would never send off for his own bride with whatever he had in his past hanging over his head. Looking back, we really shouldn't have done it without knowing what that thing was, but it was kind of a rash decision."

Clarence stepped forward then, his eyes full of remorse. "Riley, I told you once I didn't want you to live the way I have. I shouldn't have done it, and I know that, but I guess I couldn't help myself."

A hundred different emotions passed over Riley's face, but finally he placed his hand on the seasoned cowhand's shoulder. "You're both forgiven, and thank you for meddling and bringing me the best thing in my life."

Both Clarence and Joshua breathed sighs of relief at that, and Liam broke the sweet moment with a guffaw. "Why didn't you two send off for brides yourselves?"

"Joshua's got some more maturin' to do first," Clarence groused. "And I might've, but Mrs. Miller's age cutoff is forty." He shrugged, mumbling something about infernal age restrictions while the rest of them joined Liam in laughter.

Well, that was solved. As Riley took Paige back into his arms and kissed her head once again, she realized how deeply at home she felt there in his arms. Yes, only God knew what the future would hold, but beyond any doubt, Paige knew Riley would be in hers.

Just then, Coralee's high pitched, "Uncle Riley," cut through the revelry. She closed the distance between the train platform and the mercantile's front porch at a dead run, Timothy moving as fast as his little legs would carry him behind her. Lizzie and Paul followed, grins wide, as Riley released Paige and ran to swoop up both his niece and nephew at once.

As he spun them around there in the street, Paige couldn't help but think how the joy radiated from him. Now that the trial didn't hang over his head, it was as though the weight of the world no longer rested on his shoulders. "Thank You, Lord," she whispered as she approached their little group. "Thank You."

Chapter Nineteen

Christmas Eve brought a large enough snow that the whole lot of them had gotten snowed in at the Pratt ranch after sharing dinner that evening. Paul and Lizzie's family, Paul's parents, Mrs. Jacobs, Liam and Mara, Stew, Paige, and all those who normally resided on the Pratt ranch sat in front of the crackling fireplace as Samuel read the story of Jesus's birth.

Thankfully, Samuel and Kate had enough rooms that there'd been no issue housing everyone, and Riley had already moved into the house they'd share once they married. He'd wanted to do the last of the work himself, and Paige knew he'd been hard at work every spare hour he had for the last month.

Samuel closed the Bible and led them all in a prayer of thanks for everything the Lord had brought them that year. Samuel and Kate had announced at dinner that night they were expecting their first child in the summer, and Paige couldn't be more thrilled for her friend. Liam and Mara likely wouldn't be too far behind them, and Paige couldn't wait for the day she and Riley would welcome their own little ones.

If only he'd propose. He'd said he had no plans for a long engagement, but he wanted the cabin to be completely finished before he popped the question. The last time she'd been out there, it was pretty cold as the gaps between the logs hadn't yet been filled with chinking. From what she knew, that had been what he'd been working on, but it had been a week or so since she'd visited.

"And finally Lord," Samuel prayed. "Thank you for the newest member of our family. Paige came to us in a way no one expected, but You knew she belonged here. As she and my brother Riley build their own life together, we ask you'd bless them both with grace for one another, good health, and the wisdom to follow You in all things. Amen."

As everyone opened their eyes, Paige gasped at the sight of Riley down on one knee before her. He held out a ring, the grin on his face a mile wide. "Paige Brown, I never imagined a woman like you could be real. Your kindness, your compassion, your beauty - it's almost too much for a man to believe. But most of all, you helped me trust Jesus in a lifetime of fear. You're my Red Sea road, the one the Lord used to lead me into His plan for me. I reckon, if a woman can make you love the Lord more, you oughta marry her, so that's what I plan to do. Will you let me do what I should've done the day you stepped off the train and make you Mrs. Paige Hart?"

There was no way Paige could've held back the tears that flowed down her cheeks then, so she let them flow with a sob. "I thought you'd never ask."

Epilogue

January 1886

Paige fussed with the fur wrap Lizzie had lent her and picked imaginary lint from her wedding dress. She and Mara stood outside the church doors with Liam, the cold air crackling with anticipation. Why couldn't she just run up the aisle now? Paige had never sought the center of attention, and all she really wanted was to lay eyes on Riley and feel his strong hands take hers.

Liam placed a hand on each of the sisters' shoulders. "You ready for this, Paige? We can always go in and say you got lost on the way here." He winked, familiar smirk in place. "I could even say Mara kidnapped you if you wish."

With a snort, Mara elbowed her husband in the ribs. "You think you're funny."

"I know I am," Liam replied before turning serious for once. "But really Paige, one word from you, and I'll handle everything. Are you sure?"

It had been a long time since Paige had had a man in her corner to protect her. Hope House had been primarily run by women, and they'd never had any older brothers. His concern was welcome, despite it not being necessary. "I've never been more sure of anything in my life."

"Whew," Liam feigned relief. "I may be the sheriff, but Riley's strong as an ox from all the ranch work, and I didn't want to have to hold him back from going to find you."

Just then, Samuel opened the church doors, and the sound of the wedding march wafted from the piano. The pews were full of friends who'd become family, but Paige only had eyes for the man at the end of the aisle. Riley looked so handsome in the suit he'd borrowed from Samuel, and his gaze held hers like the two of them were connected by something much deeper than simple feelings.

Mara squeezed Paige's arm and kissed her cheek. "You look beautiful, little sister, and I'm so proud of you. You deserve this." Uncharacteristic tears flowed down Mara's cheeks, but Paige's were dry for once.

"Thank you for being everything for me," she whispered back. Mara turned then and headed down the aisle to take her place as Paige's matron-of-honor. Joshua already stood with Riley, as they'd decided to just have one person each stand up with them. Samuel and Kate had graciously provided much of the food for their reception, with Paul and Lizzie supplying the rest.

Pastor Martin nodded for her to step forward, his handsome face happy performing his first wedding in Mud Lake. Maybe the man would send away for his own bride before too long, but Paige had eyes for no one but her groom. Riley's smile grew impossibly bigger as she took her first steps, with her arm threaded through Liam's.

She'd finally gotten to wear the wedding dress Mrs. Miller had sent, the highly impractical lacy concoction made of delicate white fabric. Some variation of the dress was sent with each of Mrs. Miller's brides, her obsession with Queen Victoria's white wedding gown somewhat of a legend at that point. Still, as silly as she thought it was when she'd shoved it into her satchel in New Orleans, seeing the awe on Riley's face was everything she'd never realized she wanted.

Somehow, the church aisle felt a mile long, but at last, she reached the man she'd grown to love despite circumstances doing their best to pull them apart. The Lord had been faithful beyond her wildest dreams, drawing them together and to Himself. As Liam placed her hand in Riley's, it was as though any jitters melted away.

His amber eyes, captivating from the moment she met him, drew her in just like they had that day in the mercantile. Silently, he squeezed her hand and mouthed, *I love you*. His eyes misted a little, and she could see him fighting to keep the tears back. No one else could see it, but she could, and that thought warmed her. They had no secrets from one another, and he could read her like a book. She'd spend her life doing the same for him, and it would be the best book she'd ever read.

I love you, too, she mouthed back. Pastor Martin started speaking, but Paige wasn't quite as focused as she ought to be. No, it was as though Riley had crowded all her senses, but she couldn't complain. Just before she forced herself to listen to the pastor so as not to miss her cue to speak, Riley winked, and an overwhelming sense of gratitude washed over her.

Their first days hadn't been as she might've wished, but it turned out, the Lord knew what He was doing after all. Had Clarence and Joshua not sent off that letter, how different would her life look right now? There was no way to know, but one thing was certain. She was home, exactly where she needed to be. Anticipation for the future filled her in a way she couldn't explain if she tried, and for the first time in her life, the uncertainty was full of hope.

Want more from Riley, Paige, and the whole Hope House family? Check out this bonus epilogue! For paperback readers, shoot me an email at maloryfordbooks@gmail.com , and I'll be happy to send you the exclusively e-epilogue.

Have you read my other two books set in the world of Hope House? Grab the Legacy Series and the Waymaker series today!

About the Author

Malory is a wife and mother, avid gardener, aspiring baker, and a voracious reader.

She is a believer inspired by everyday encounters with the Lord, interactions with her friends and family, and the occasional trip into a history book.

Made in the USA
Coppell, TX
21 June 2024

33761085R00132